for a long moment.

"Do you love me, Lucas?" she asked quietly.

"It doesn't matter."

"Of course it matters. It means everything."

He shook his head. "No. What matters is that this is no kind of life for you. I've seen what it's done to other people. I've seen how it's hardened me. I don't want that to happen to you. You have such a loving heart. You deserve a lot more than life here can offer you."

Kara had to fight back her tears. "I want to stay with you."

He looked straight into her eyes. "No."

"I love you."

Dear Reader,

August is vacation month, and no matter where you're planning to go, don't forget to take along this month's Silhouette Romance novels. They're the perfect summertime read! And even if you can't get away, you can still escape from it all for a few hours of love and adventure with Silhouette Romance books.

August continues our WRITTEN IN THE STARS series. Each month in 1992 we're proud to present a book that focuses on the hero and his astrological sign. This month we're featuring the proud, passionate Leo man in Suzanne Carey's intensely emotional *Baby Swap.*

You won't want to miss the rest of our fabulous August lineup. We have love stories by Elizabeth August, Brittany Young, Carol Grace and Carla Cassidy. As a special treat, we're introducing a talented newcomer, Sandra Paul. And in months to come, watch for Silhouette Romance novels by many more of your favorite authors, including Diana Palmer, Annette Broadrick and Marie Ferrarella.

The Silhouette Romance authors and editors love to hear from readers and we'd love to hear from *you.*

Happy reading from all of us at Silhouette!

Valerie Susan Hayward
Senior Editor

BRITTANY YOUNG

A Holiday To Remember

Silhouette Romance
Published by Silhouette Books New York
America's Publisher of Contemporary Romance

To the rhino man, Michael Werikhe, for his efforts in saving African wildlife and for his inspiration to me.

SILHOUETTE BOOKS
300 E. 42nd St., New York, N.Y. 10017

A HOLIDAY TO REMEMBER

ISBN: 0-373-08885-X

First Silhouette Books printing August 1992

Printed in the U.S.A.

Books by Brittany Young

Silhouette Romance

Arranged Marriage #165
A Separate Happiness #297
No Special Consideration #308
The Karas Cup #336
An Honorable Man #357
A Deeper Meaning #375
No Ordinary Man #388
To Catch a Thief #424
Gallagher's Lady #454
All or Nothing #484
Far from Over #537
A Matter of Honor #550
Worth the Risk #574
The Kiss of a Stranger #597
A Man Called Travers #622
The White Rose #640
A Woman in Love #658
The Ambassador's Daughter #700
The Seduction of Anna #729
The House by the Lake #759
One Man's Destiny #807
Lady in Distress #831
A Holiday To Remember #885

Silhouette Books

Silhouette Christmas Stories 1989
"Silent Night"

BRITTANY YOUNG

lives and writes in Racine, Wisconsin. She has traveled to most of the countries that serve as the settings for her books and finds the research into the language, customs, history and literature of these countries among the most demanding and rewarding aspects of her writing.

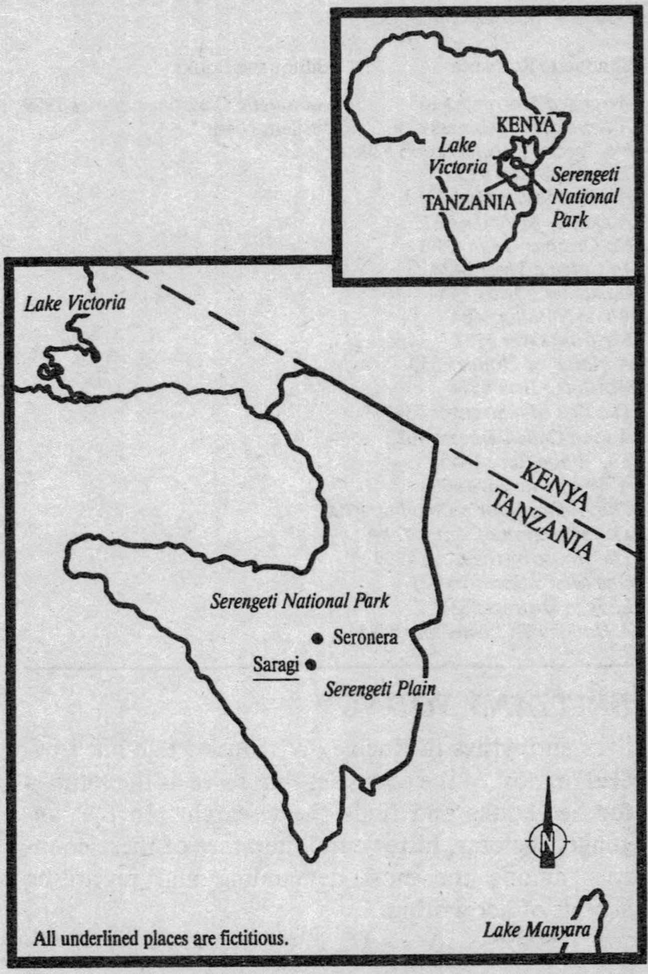
KENYA
Lake
Victoria
Serengeti
National
Park
TANZANIA
Lake Victoria
KENYA
TANZANIA
Serengeti National Park
Seronera
Saragi
Serengeti Plain
N
Lake Manyara
All underlined places are fictitious.

Chapter One

Dr. Lucas Pierson stepped onto the veranda and stood at the head of the stairs. Taking off his battered bush hat, he drew his forearm across his perspiring forehead and squinted into the bright African sun. Lines creased the corners of his blue eyes as he scanned the skies for his plane.

"Joe's late getting back," said his partner in the game reserve, the screen door banging shut as he came out of the house.

"It's probably because of those damn people he had to pick up. I don't know why we agreed to let them come here in the first place. This is a working reserve, not a vacation spot for the rich and bored."

"We're doing it because we need the money," Craig said bluntly. "And they're willing to pay us handsomely to host them for a few weeks."

The muscle in Lucas's jaw tightened. "It galls me," he said quietly in his Australian drawl, "this incessant begging for funds."

"I know, but it's been a fact of our lives for the past ten years. We knew that when we came out here."

There was a metallic glint in the distant sky. "That must be them," Lucas said.

They stood in silence as the plane dropped lower in the sky and prepared to land on the flat plain that stretched as far as the eye could see.

"Let's go meet them," Craig said. "And be charming. Maybe they'll be willing to donate something extra. We've got to get a new truck pretty soon."

Lucas put his hat on. "You be charming," he said as he started down the steps. "I'm going back to work. Tell Joe to put the supplies in the shed."

Craig shook his head as he watched his friend climb into a Range Rover and drive off, leaving a cloud of dust. The two men had known each other since childhood, so he was used to Lucas's impatience and was rarely offended by it. They worked well together, each man having his own particular strengths. For Lucas, saving the animals of the Serengeti was his life. Because man was the enemy of the animals he'd come to care so deeply about, man had become Lucas's enemy as well. He no longer bothered to disguise his contempt.

That's where Craig came in. He had a natural charm. He knew how to use it and did so, often and without apology. It was because of his charm and his ability to wheedle money out of the most unlikely people that this reserve and the wildlife preservation work going on here was able to continue. He was proud of that fact.

The plane touched down and rolled across the dry, waving grass to a stop about five hundred yards away. Whistling cheerily, Craig climbed into his own battered Range Rover and drove to meet it. He got there just as the first woman was climbing to the ground and hurried to help her.

"Hello," he said with a wide smile as he took the woman's small white hand in his and helped her from the plane.

She looked up at him with wide blue eyes. The tiniest of smiles hovered at the corners of her rosebud mouth. "Hello," she said softly.

"Welcome to Saragi. I'm Craig Johnson. And you are?"

"Quinn Whitcomb." She tucked her short, very blond hair behind her ear.

Another woman looked out of the plane's door. Her thick reddish-gold hair fell in unruly ringlets to her shoulders.

"This is my sister, Kara Stanhope," Quinn said as she looked back at the plane.

Kara grinned at him. "Hi."

Craig grinned, too, as he reached out to help her down. "Hi yourself."

"You must be Dr. Pierson."

"I'm afraid not. I'm his partner, Craig Johnson."

"Oh, excuse me," she said as she took his hand and jumped to the ground. "I understood that we were to be met by Dr. Pierson."

Kara could see that her innocent remark made the man uncomfortable and she wondered why.

Craig cleared his throat. "I'm afraid Lucas had something pressing to take care of. Very pressing. Things are constantly cropping up around here, as you can imagine. Constantly. One thing after another."

Kara had always found it easy to read people. She arched her eyebrow in an all-too-clear understanding of why Lucas Pierson wasn't there. "Oh, dear," she said, more amused than offended, "to put an American twist on Shakespeare, you're protesting way too much."

Craig definitely liked this woman. "Damn," he said with mock seriousness, "I knew it even as I was saying it. I should have stopped right after telling you he had something pressing to take care of."

Kara nodded. "If I were editing your conversation, that's where I would have stopped."

Quinn looked from one to the other, obviously wondering what on earth the two of them were talking about.

"Well, that does leave me with something of a problem," Craig said. "Where do we go from here? Conversationally speaking, of course."

"You could start by telling us the real reason Dr. Pierson isn't here," Kara suggested.

"I don't think so," Craig said, shaking his head. "That wouldn't be very diplomatic of me."

"We're big girls, Mr. Johnson. I think we can take the truth, right, Quinn?"

"Leave me out of this. I haven't the slightest idea what the two of you are talking about."

Craig shrugged. "All right, the truth is that Lucas doesn't much care for tourists."

A smile tugged at the corners of Kara's mouth. "Just our money."

"You understand completely."

"Completely."

"For heaven's sake, Bertie, give me a hand." A heavyset woman filled the door of the plane.

"I'm trying, my love, but I can't get through."

"Must I do everything myself?"

Craig moved quickly to the woman and held his hand up. "May I help you?"

She looked him up and down and put out her hands to rest on his shoulders. Craig, his face red from the effort, swung her to the ground.

"Thank you, young man. Bertie? Bertie! Stop dawdling and come on out."

"Yes, dear."

Bertie, as skinny as his wife was large, his shoulders slightly stooped, took Craig's proffered hand and jumped to the ground.

The woman put her hands on her hips and looked around. "Not very impressive so far," she finally said. "I hope your accommodations are better than the last hellhole we were at."

"Now, Hilda," her husband said, "it wasn't that bad."

"Don't contradict me, Bertie. It most certainly was."

Kara and Quinn looked at each other with mutual sympathy. It had been a close fit in the little plane for the four of them plus the pilot, and Hilda and Bertie had bickered throughout the entire two-hour flight.

"And this heat! It's like an inferno out here. Bertie, where's my hat?"

The little man reached into the plane and came out with a hard brimmed jungle hat that he handed to his wife. She put it on and pressed a switch that activated a little battery-powered fan on the front of it while everyone watched in amazement. "That's a little better," she said after a moment, "but not much. I trust our quarters here are air-conditioned."

"I regret to say they're not," Craig said politely.

"What? Why not?"

"That's a luxury we can't afford, but I'm sure you'll like your rooms. They're very comfortable. And I think you'll find the evenings are cool."

"They'd better be, young man. Come, Bertie." She strode to the Range Rover with Bertie right behind her.

Craig looked at Kara and Quinn. "You're not with them, are you? Tell me you're not with them."

"We just met them at the airport this morning," Quinn said in her whispery voice.

Craig looked from one sister to the other. They couldn't have been more different. Where Kara's skin was tanned and glowing, Quinn's was ghostly pale.

Kara was probably five foot eight to Quinn's five foot two, and while Kara was slender, she looked positively robust next to Quinn's ethereal thinness. They were both beautiful.

"Joe," Craig said as he dragged his gaze from them to speak to the pilot, "help me with the luggage. After we drop everyone off at the house, you can take the supplies to the shed and unload them."

"Right."

"Be careful with my makeup case, young man," Hilda called from the Range Rover as Joe removed a rather large carry case from the plane.

"Yes, ma'am," he said politely as he placed it gently in the Rover.

"What was the fire line like when you flew over it?" Craig asked the pilot.

"It's a long one, but not moving toward us very fast. I'd say it's still at least two weeks away."

"Good. The rains will probably put it out before it gets this far. But make sure you talk to Lucas about it anyway when he gets back."

Kara had been listening with interest. She'd seen the spectacular wall of fire from the air. "Is it dangerous to us here at Saragi?"

"Not if we keep an eye on it. We have fires here all through the dry season. If it gets too close, there are steps we can take to protect ourselves and the buildings."

"You sound so casual about it."

"It comes from a decade of living out here. There aren't too many things we haven't been through."

Kara nodded her understanding as she looked around. "Is that where we'll be staying?" she asked, her eyes alighting on the house with the veranda.

Craig's gaze followed her own. "Yes. That's the main house. We all have rooms there." He gestured toward the car. "Your chariot, ladies."

"I think we'll walk, if you don't mind. We've been sitting for days." Kara looked at her sister. "Is that all right with you, Quinn?"

"Sure," she said quietly.

Kara smiled at Craig. "We'll meet you there. And, Joe, thank you for flying us here."

The pilot, handsome and young, winked at her and went on with his unloading.

"What's the story with those two?" Craig asked as he watched the two young women walking away arm in arm.

"I only know what I heard them talking about in the plane," Joe said with a grunt as he lifted a heavy box. "It sounded to me like the one named Quinn lost her husband or something like that, had a bout with depression and came out here to get over it."

"What do you mean she lost her husband? You make it sound like she misplaced him."

"He died."

"Died?" he said in surprise. "That's really a shame. She's so young."

"Yeah."

"What about the tall one?" Craig asked, his eyes still on the women.

"As far as I can tell, she's just here to take care of her sister." Joe slapped him on the back to get his attention. "Hey, a little help already. You can look at them later."

A few minutes later, Kara took a deep breath as she and Quinn walked. It smelled like—earth. "Now that we've been here for all of ten minutes," she said to her sister, "what do you think so far?"

Quinn wrinkled her nose in distaste. "I think it's hot. Very, very hot."

Kara laughed. "You sound like Hilda. We'll have to buy you one of those hats."

"Oh, heavens, anything but that!"

Kara's smile faded. "Really, though, do you think you're going to like it here?"

"The short answer is no, I don't think I'm going to like it here at all."

"What's the long answer?"

Quinn stopped walking and looked around with a sigh that came from deep inside her. "It certainly is away from everything and everyone, isn't it?"

She sounded so forlorn it nearly broke Kara's heart. "That's the whole point, honey."

"I know." Quinn stared at the house. It seemed large enough, but it looked so—*basic*—and so sad sitting in the middle of this horrid patch of nowhere. She could see other wood structures beyond the house that no reputable architect of her acquaintance would call buildings. Some had thatched roofs, some corrugated tin. There was no lawn or flowers. Just grass the color of hay, and dust.

Lots of dust.

The light breeze lifted it from the ground and glued it to her unhappily perspiring body. Even the scattered acacia trees with their distinctive flat tops failed to brighten the landscape. Quinn was very much an urban creature who liked to be as comfortable as modern technology could make her. This didn't look promising at all. "I hate it already," she finally said.

Kara gazed at the same surroundings and her heart sank. Primitive was a word that came to mind, and even that might have been a kindness. She tried to look on the bright side. The wood house had certainly seen better days, but the veranda that wound around it with its tattered furniture had a certain charm—if one used one's imagination. The Serengeti Plain spread out in all directions like a field of golden wheat.

Yes, she thought, that was a good way of seeing it. A field of golden wheat with the leaves of the acacias bright, exotic splashes of green. There were rock formations—huge boulders stacked by nature, worn smooth by the centuries—scattered around like odd works of ancient art.

"What do you think?" Quinn asked, watching her sister closely. "And be honest. Don't tell me what you think I want to hear."

Kara forced a bright smile on her face. "Well, it certainly is . . . unique."

"Unique? That's the best you can do? You, the eternal optimist?"

"Just give me a minute. I'll do better." Kara thought quickly. "All right. I've got it. Despite the way things look at the moment, our time here is going to be a wonderful growth experience for us. A time we can take back to Chicago with us, with the knowledge that we're better people for..."

"Having survived," Quinn finished for her.

Kara's green eyes twinkled. "Exactly."

The two of them looked at each other and burst out laughing.

"Well," Quinn said after a minute, "at least we're together. Whose brilliant idea was this, anyway?"

"You can take full credit."

"Temporary insanity. That's my only excuse. We could have gone to Rome or Paris."

"They would have just meant more sad memories of places you were with your husband. This is completely off the path of your normal life. It's the perfect place for you right now. Here you can begin to move on with your life and start creating new memories with new people."

"I suppose." She squeezed Kara's arm. "In case I haven't mentioned it, it was good of you to come with me. I'd never have done this by myself."

"I wouldn't have had it any other way."

Quinn stood there, lost in thought, as the Rover moved past them. "Have you ever been in love, Kara?"

Kara didn't have to think about her answer. It was something that had been on her mind more and more lately. "Unfortunately, no," she said softly. "There have been men I've liked very much—and even some I was quite fond of, in a sisterly sort of way. But I've never really been in love."

"Oh, don't say unfortunately, Kara. As far as I'm concerned, you're one of the lucky ones. I can't imagine anything worse than loving someone and losing them."

Kara disagreed with her sister, but she didn't argue with her. Now wasn't the time.

"Besides," Quinn said, warming to her topic, "how do you know you haven't been in love? You've never let a man get close enough for you to find out."

"They don't have to get close. I'll know the right man for me when I meet him."

Quinn shook her head. "You're such a romantic. It doesn't work that way."

"Perhaps not for everyone." Kara wasn't defensive, just matter-of-fact. She'd always believed in destiny. It was what kept her looking forward to life with such anticipation.

Kara and Quinn, standing arm in arm, looked at the house.

"Well," Kara said after a moment, "shall we go see what wonderful surprises await us?"

"Bugs, reptiles, creatures with big teeth . . ." Quinn shivered. "Yech."

"There are bugs, reptiles and creatures with big teeth in Chicago, too. And in Rome and Paris, for that matter."

"Oh, that makes me feel a lot better."

"Well, most of those are of the two-legged variety," she said dryly. "At least out here, what you see is what you get. No surprises."

Just as they reached the steps, Craig walked around the corner of the veranda. "Well, I've settled the Griffins in their room."

He picked up their two suitcases as Kara shouldered both her carry-on bag and Quinn's.

"Thanks. Follow me, ladies. Through there," he said as he inclined his head toward a screen door, "is our combined living, dining, game and generally whatever-you-want-to-use-it-for room. We meet in there every morning at six-thirty for breakfast and every evening at eight for dinner."

Quinn's eyes widened. "Breakfast at six-thirty a.m.?"

"That's right."

"How uncivilized. I'm never up at that hour. I'll have to have my breakfast served later."

"No can do. You either eat with the rest of us or fend for yourself." He turned the corner on the veranda and Kara saw that the house was much larger than she'd at first supposed.

"This is my room," he said as he passed the first screen door, "and this is the Griffins," he said of the next screen door. "You're in here, Quinn." He opened the third screen door and stepped aside so the two women could enter.

Kara followed Quinn inside and looked around the sparsely furnished room in silent distress. It contained the bare minimum of furniture: a bed with four posters to hold the mosquito netting, a dresser and a small desk. A paddle fan slowly rotated in the middle of the ceiling, barely stirring the hot air.

"Oh, my," Quinn said as she sank dejectedly onto the bed.

"Which suitcase is yours?" Craig asked.

She looked up at him blankly. "Excuse me?"

"The suitcases. Which one is yours?"

"Oh. The black one."

He set it beside the wall and turned back to her. "Look," he said kindly, "I know it doesn't look like much, but the place will grow on you, trust me."

She smiled at him, but it was a quavery one.

He then turned to Kara. "And you're right next door. I'm sure you could find it on your own, but good host that I am, I'll take you." He carried her suitcase to a room exactly like Quinn's and set it down. "Lucas's room is on the other side of yours, and on the other side of his room is the bathroom."

"*The* bathroom?" Kara asked. "There's just one? For all of us?"

"Well, there's another about twenty feet from the house. That's just a shower. It's a little on the public side. The men around here usually use that one. I think you and your sister might prefer the relative privacy of the one here at the house."

"One bathroom," Kara said with a half smile. "Welcome to Africa. Are you going to tell Quinn or am I?" she asked.

"Not me. I only bring people good news."

"Gotcha."

"Of course, there's a basin and bottled water in your closet for quick cleanups."

Kara sighed.

"I'll admit, it's not exactly the Ritz."

"The Ritz? Are you kidding?" she said dryly.

Craig laughed, then his smile faded. "Your sister doesn't much like it here, does she?" he asked, completely ignoring the fact that Kara wasn't exactly thrilled, either.

Kara studied his rather ordinary but very kind face and found herself wanting to reassure him. "She'll be all right, Craig. This is just very, very different from what she's used to."

"I can imagine. She seems so..."

"Delicate?" Kara suggested with an inward sigh. Men always assumed that Quinn was delicate and Kara was strong. The two of them had sort of slipped into those roles over the years.

"Yes." He nodded. "Delicate."

"That's because she's so tiny."

Craig shifted to his other foot, uncharacteristically shy all of a sudden. "Uh, Joe said something about her losing her husband."

"About a year ago."

"I'm sorry."

"We all are. Steven was a fine man."

"How's she doing?"

"About as well as can be expected. Depression has been a problem for her. That's why we came out here. We thought perhaps a change of scenery..." Kara's voice faded as she studied the man in front of her. Interesting, she thought. Very, very interesting.

"Sure," he said, nodding. "I understand. We'll take real good care of her. You have my word on it."

Kara smiled at him, suddenly sensing the possibilities.

Craig smiled back, blissfully unaware that he was a marked man. He looked at his watch. "It's only six, so you can wash up and have a rest before dinner if you'd like."

"I'd rather wander around, if you don't mind. I've never been on a game reserve before. And if you have the time, I'm sure Quinn would appreciate your showing her how things work around here."

Craig hesitated. "I'm afraid I don't have time right now. You can look around on your own, but use your common sense and don't leave the grounds. It's too easy to get lost."

"All right."

"And after dinner we'll talk about what you, your sister and the Griffins want to do for the next couple of weeks."

"Thanks."

Craig turned around to leave the room and almost ran into Quinn as she entered. "Whoa!" he said with a smile as he backed up a step. "Sorry about that. See you at dinner, Quinn."

She waited until he was out of earshot. "This is awful, Kara. Just awful. I mean, I was ready for some inconveniences, but have you looked around this place? It's horrible!"

"You think this is bad? Wait until I tell you about the bathroom setup."

"Oh," she groaned, "I don't want to know. I just want to go someplace civilized. I should never have come here. I shouldn't have dragged you with me."

Kara laughed as she hugged her. "Quinn, I know it's hard to believe right now, but I think this place is just what the doctor ordered."

"So you want to stay?" she asked incredulously. "You actually want to stay here?"

"Yes, I do. I can't really explain it, but I have a feeling about Saragi. A good feeling. And besides, I spent a small fortune to get myself out here. I want to go home with something more than a case of heat rash."

Quinn favored her sister with a reluctant smile. "Well, it's only for three weeks. I suppose I can manage."

"I predict that you'll not only manage, you'll thrive."

"Let's not get carried away."

"You'll see. What do you say we unpack and then go exploring?" Kara asked as she swung her suitcase onto the bed.

"Exploring? As in wandering around the great outdoors unprotected with the rest of God's creatures?"

"That's the general idea."

"Not me. No way."

"Oh, come on. Just for a little while."

Quinn shook her head. "To tell you the truth, I'm a little tired. I think I'll take a nap."

"All right. I'll wake you before dinner."

"Thanks."

As Quinn left, Kara put her clothes neatly into the drawers and closet. She'd purposely kept her packing to a minimum. When she was finished, she zipped the suitcase shut and slid it under the bed. Looking down at the full marine-blue-and-brown print skirt she had on, Kara debated for a moment about whether or not to change her clothes and decided to stay the way she was.

Except for her hair. Her miserable, unruly hair.

Kara spotted a small mirror tacked to the wall above the dresser. She leaned over to look at herself and grimaced.

Grabbing a brush, she dragged it through her hair and pulled the thick curls into a ponytail that she caught low at the back of her neck with a blue ribbon. One of these days she was going to cut it all off. Whack it. No mercy.

Tossing the brush onto the dresser top, she walked outside. The screen door slammed shut behind her.

She crossed the veranda to the railing and looked around. The sun was less intense now, but she could still see waves of heat rising from the plain, blurring the view in the distance. And she could hear animal noises.

Animal noises?

Following the trail of grunts and screeches, Kara walked around the veranda to the back of the house and into a different world. Straight out from the house about fifty feet away was an entire village of animals. Kara couldn't believe her eyes. Fenced pens, lean-tos, and walled shelters with a wide dirt avenue running through the middle of them.

There were gazelles wandering in the avenue, not the least bit afraid of her. Several monkeys perched on the bare branch of an acacia near one of the pens, chattering madly.

Kara was enchanted. She stepped down from the veranda and crossed to the first pen. Its sole occupant, an ostrich, stood in the far corner watching her with its huge eyes.

"You look like a Mabel," Kara said with a smile.

The ostrich blinked, lowering lids with some of the most outrageously long eyelashes she'd ever seen.

"I know women who'd kill for eyelashes like that," she said dryly as she looked the ostrich over. A large taped area on her right thigh seemed to be coming loose at the top. Kara walked around the pen to the gate and opened it, speaking softly as she moved toward the ostrich. "Don't be frightened, Mabel. I'm just going to fix your bandage."

The ostrich started pacing.

Kara cautiously moved closer. "I'm not going to hurt you. Stand still."

The ostrich suddenly ran at her.

Kara screamed, turned toward the gate to run away and stumbled. Strong arms closed around her, lifted her off her feet and set her roughly to one side as the ostrich dashed past.

"Kito! Lado! Catch her!" boomed a low voice with an Australian accent.

Kara, her back against the fence where she'd been summarily deposited, watched as two African men came running across the compound toward the terrified ostrich. The man who'd grabbed her had his broad back toward her. He and the other two men formed a circle around the large bird. It ran at the shorter of the two African men. He stepped quickly backward. The other two men quickly closed the circle again, narrowing it more and more until the ostrich had nowhere to run. Then they opened up one end of the circle and herded the bird back into the pen.

The Australian grabbed Kara's arm and jerked her out of the pen as the other men closed and latched the gate.

Furious blue eyes bored into her. "What the hell do you think you're doing?"

Kara swallowed hard. He was really intimidating. "I was just trying to help. The bandage on her leg seemed to be coming loose."

"So you, with all of your glorious medical wisdom, thought you'd fix it?"

"Well, I..."

"The bandage is exactly the way it's supposed to be. Do you have any idea of the kind of damage that ostrich could have inflicted on you? Not to mention the rest of us?"

Kara couldn't believe what she was hearing. "Oh, for heaven's sake, it's an ostrich, not a lion. How could Mabel possibly hurt anyone?"

The man was clearly caught off guard. "Mabel?"

"She looks like a Mabel, don't you think?" Kara turned to examine the ostrich.

"As it happens, your gentle—Mabel is it?"

Kara nodded.

"Your gentle Mabel has a claw on the back of each foot that could slice you wide open from your chin to your ankles. When they can run away, it's not a problem. But when they're cornered, they fight."

Kara felt duly chastised—not to mention incredibly stupid. "I'm really sorry. I had no idea."

"Perhaps next time you'll think twice before walking into a cage with a wild animal."

"I will. I didn't mean to cause any trouble." She extended her hand. "I'm Kara Stanhope. You must be Dr. Pierson."

He looked at her hand for a moment before extending his own to capture hers in a firm grip. "Lucas. We don't stand on formalities around here."

Kara smiled but he didn't smile back.

Her smile faded and she cleared her throat, embarrassed. Her charms were obviously wasted on this guy.

"From now on, stay away from the animals unless you're with someone who knows what they're doing."

"I will."

He turned to leave.

"May I ask you something?" Kara said.

Lucas looked at his watch. "If you make it brief."

"What will you do with Mabel when she's healed?"

"We'll release her back into the wild in the same place we found her."

"And she'll be all right?"

"I know my job, Miss Stanhope."

"Of course, you do. I didn't mean to imply anything—" Kara cut herself off and sighed. "I have this horrible, sinking feeling that I'm going to be doing a lot of apologizing during the next three weeks."

"You, of course, would know best about that." He looked at his watch again. "And now, if you'll excuse me, I have other things to attend to."

Kara watched him walk away. Now that she was no longer confronted with those blue eyes, she could notice other things about him, such as how tall he was. Perhaps six foot four or six foot five. The chambray shirt he was wearing was loose, but the strength of the body beneath the material was obvious. The name Conan came provocatively to mind. Sweat had darkened a stripe from his shoulders to his narrow, jeans-clad hips.

He was gorgeous. Arrogant, but most definitely gorgeous.

Lucas stopped on the veranda to speak with a man she hadn't seen before. Kara quickly turned away so he wouldn't catch her gawking.

Even as she turned, she saw the vividly spotted cat flying through the air, its sleek body aimed right at her. Its great paws hit her shoulders and knocked her to the ground before she could scream. Her back's contact with the solidly packed dirt knocked the air from her lungs in one great gasp. Golden cat's eyes stared into Kara's. She threw her hands up to protect her face and throat and waited for the pain that was sure to follow.

A rough tongue licked the back of her hand.

It took Kara a moment to realize that she wasn't being bitten. Cautiously she fanned open the fingers covering one eye and looked at her attacker—who was still sitting on her as though she were a favorite cushion.

It was a cheetah.

She fanned open the fingers of the other hand and stared, not moving, afraid to startle the animal.

From the corner of her eye she saw a pair of jeans-clad legs stop beside her.

Lucas clapped his hands. "Sophia, get off her. You know better than that."

The cheetah thought it over for a moment, not the least intimidated, stepped off of Kara with the attitude that she was doing it because *she* wanted to and for no other reason, and sauntered toward the house.

Kara lay in the dirt looking up at Lucas as he stood towering over her, arms akimbo. Raising her hand, she rolled her fingers in a wave and flashed her most charming smile. "Hi, there. Back so soon?"

The muscles in his jaw clenched, but Kara could have sworn she saw a hint of amusement behind his eyes. "I'm beginning to sense a pattern here."

"Now, wait a minute. You can't blame me for this one. I'm not the one who opened her cage."

"Sophia isn't kept in a cage." He grabbed her hand and pulled her to her feet in one swift motion.

"So she's a pet?" Kara asked incredulously as she dusted herself off.

"As much of a pet as a cheetah can be."

"And is this how she greets all of your guests?"

"Sophia usually ignores the guests. She's apparently taken a liking to you."

"Wait just a minute," Kara said incredulously. "Let's see if I understand this correctly. You're saying that that was an affectionate tackle?"

"You're alive, aren't you?"

A corner of her mouth lifted. "As far as I can tell."

"Then it was an affectionate tackle." Lucas put his hands on her shoulders and turned her around so he could dust off the back of her skirt. "There," he said when he'd finished and turned her again to face him. "If you don't mind a little friendly advice, I'd like to suggest that you call it a day as far as the animals go."

Kara couldn't help but smile. "You mean that I should go to my room like a good girl?"

"You can go to your room if you want, of course. Personally," he said, reaching out and rubbing some dirt from her cheek, "I think you could use a shower."

Kara blinked in surprise, then laughed at his bluntness. "Boy, you don't put a lot of effort into being likable, do you?"

"That's nothing but wasted energy." His blue eyes moved over her face. "Now, are you going to need rescuing again or can I go about my business?"

Kara was still smiling. "I think I'll be all right."

He inclined his head. "Then I'll bid you g'day."

Once again, Kara watched as Lucas walked away from her, a bemused look on her face as she absently brushed her fingers against the cheek he'd touched.

Chapter Two

Kara leaned over and looked at herself in the mirror. Lucas was right, she thought as she rubbed a streak of dirt from her chin. A shower was definitely in order.

There were some towels on the top shelf of her closet. She took one, picked up her soap, shampoo and her short green terry-cloth robe, and headed down the veranda to a louvered door. She knocked. When no one responded, she opened it a crack and looked inside.

"Oh, dear," she said softly as she stepped inside and looked around. It was certainly clean but gave new meaning to the word primitive. It was just a little larger than her closet.

There was a small sink with an old-fashioned faucet. Over the sink was a warped mirror that could have taken honors at a carnival. Kara didn't even recognize herself in it.

Leaning over the sink, she jiggled the cold-water knob. A kind of brackish, room temperature liquid came out.

She turned that one off and turned the hot-water knob. Precisely the same room-temperature water sputtered out of the faucet.

Wonderful.

There was no bathtub, but there was a curtainless shower. She looked inside.

No knobs.

Curious, she stepped inside, still dressed, and looked around. It had to be the shower. There was a shower head. There was a short chain.

A chain?

Kara tentatively tugged on it.

Nothing happened.

She tugged a little harder.

Nothing happened.

She started to get out of the shower, resigned to a sponge bath, but couldn't resist turning back and giving it one last tug. Water flew out of the shower head straight into her face, drenching her in a sudden burst. She let go of the chain and just stood there gasping, a soaking mess. A narrow stream of water flowed down her face and dripped off the end of her nose.

Kara closed her eyes and shook her head. Dumb, dumb, dumb, dumb.

But at least Lucas Pierson wasn't around to witness it this time.

Stepping outside the shower, Kara stripped off the wet clothes. They hit the tiles with a soggy slap. Taking her soap and shampoo with her, she stepped back inside, pulled on the chain and let the water run over her. It might have been lukewarm, but it felt good to get rid of the dust and sweat.

Releasing the chain, Kara hummed softly as she soaped her hair and body. She took her time, then tugged on the chain and held on to it until all of the suds had washed away. It was the first time in days of traveling that she'd felt truly relaxed.

Still humming, she reached for the frayed towel, pulled it into the shower and vigorously rubbed the water from her hair. She didn't think too much of it when her foot bumped something cool on the shower floor. Looking down, expecting to see that her soap had fallen, her heart nearly stopped when she saw a snake—a huge snake with a body that was nearly as thick as one of her legs—slithering into the shower.

"Oh, my God," she breathed in horror, frozen to the floor. She wanted to run but was afraid the snake would attack her. Did they react to noise? Could she scream? Could she *not* scream? "Help," she croaked timidly.

The snake kept slithering. It moved its cool, scaly body over her foot.

Kara's heart slammed against her ribs. "Help!" she yelled louder.

But it kept coming. Its body nearly filled the floor of the small shower.

"Help!" she screamed. "Help me, please, somebody!"

She heard a door slam and footsteps race across the wood veranda.

"I'm in the shower!" she yelled. "Hurry!"

The door crashed open and the man she least—and most—wanted to see filled the doorway.

Lucas looked at Kara in quiet resignation as she stood there clutching the scrawny towel in front of her. A mass of red curls fell in damp profusion around her shoulders. "Oh," he said as if he should have expected it. "It's you again. What is it this time?"

Kara clutched the towel more tightly to her with one hand as she pointed at the snake with the other. "On the floor," she said trying to quell her rising hysteria.

Lucas looked down at the snake, now all the way into the shower, and his teeth flashed white in his tanned face.

Kara could have slapped him. She was about to be killed by a snake and he was smiling. "Is there something about this that particularly amuses you?" she asked, her anger overtaking her fear.

"There's nothing to be afraid of. Old Julius is harmless enough. He won't hurt you."

Kara looked incredulously from Lucas to the snake. "You're on a first-name basis with this reptile?"

"Julius Squeezer. He's our pet boa constrictor."

Her eyes were locked onto the snake. "This is a pet?"

"We let him have the run of the place. He's good for keeping pests away."

"I think there's a message in there somewhere for me, but I'll have to give it some deeper thought later. Right now I just want this thing away from me. Far, far away from me."

"He was probably attracted by the moisture."

"Get him out of here!" she said, her voice rising. "Please! I can take ostriches running at me. I can even handle being mugged by a cheetah. But this is a snake. I draw the line at snakes."

"Come on, Julius," Lucas said as he reached for the boa constrictor. "The lady wants to shower alone."

Kara backed into a corner of the shower and watched in horrified fascination as he casually looped the snake several times around his shoulders.

"If you don't want him in here showering with you in the future," Lucas said, eyeing her, "you'll have to latch the door. If it's open even a crack, he'll get in."

"Thank you for the advice," she said tightly. "Where are you going to take him?"

"Under the porch."

"Porch? This porch? The one that runs around the house?"

"Yes. That's where he lives."

"But he doesn't have to live there, does he?" she asked hopefully. "Couldn't he live under a different porch?"

Lucas smiled at her, but it wasn't a friendly smile. There was something in it that spoke more clearly than words of his disdain for her; of his certainty that she was weak and silly and would never be able to go the distance out here—not even for three short weeks. "This is his home," he said of the boa constrictor. "You, on the other hand, are free to leave at any time." With an inclination of his dark blond head, he walked out with the snake.

Well, that tore it as far as Kara was concerned. No more complaints. No more whining. No more fear. If Lucas Pierson thought he was going to chase her away after she'd gone to all the trouble of getting here in the first place, he had another think coming.

And there was also a matter of personal pride.

He was so smug.

But he wouldn't be when she was finished with him. From this moment forward, she was going to handle anything and everything that was thrown her way. And she'd handle it cheerfully. She'd show him what she was made of.

Still angry, she roughly rubbed her skin with the towel until it was pink. Stepping out of the shower, she slipped on her robe and tied the belt, scooped up her things and went determinedly to her room.

Kara sifted through her closet. She didn't have the slightest idea what one wore to dinner at a game reserve. Nothing too dressy, certainly. She finally decided on white linen trousers that had held up surprising well considering how long they'd been packed, a short-sleeved linen camp shirt and a wide green belt. She left her hair alone, except for a quick brushing that did absolutely nothing to tame her curls.

Before leaving her room, she took a deep, calming breath, put a smile on her face and opened her door. There was no one else on the veranda as she made her way to her sister's room.

"Quinn?" she said, peering in through the screen door. "Are you ready for dinner?"

"Come on in, Kara. I don't think I want any dinner."

Kara opened her sister's door and walked over to the bed. "Are you feeling all right?" she asked softly.

Quinn smiled up at her. "Don't look so worried. I'm fine. Just tired."

"But you really should eat something."

"I'm not hungry."

Kara didn't say anything for a moment. It was hard to know when to push Quinn and when to back off. She finally decided to back off. "Would you like me to bring you some dinner here?"

"No, thank you."

Kara pushed Quinn's hair away from her forehead as though she were a child. Even though Kara was the younger sister, she'd always been very protective of Quinn. Life seemed to take so much more of a toll on her. "All right. I'll leave you in peace. But tomorrow we're going exploring together. You wouldn't believe the trouble I've been getting into on my own."

"You?" Quinn said with a tired smile. "I'm shocked. Since when do high school English teachers get into trouble?"

"Since this particular one arrived here."

"I can't imagine why you'd think I can keep you out of trouble, but if I feel all right I'll wander around with you tomorrow."

"Good." Kara headed for the door. "I'll check on you before I go to bed."

"Don't wake me if I'm asleep."

"I won't." Kara opened the door, but hesitated. "Are you sure you're all right?"

"I'm sure," Quinn said softly. "Please don't worry so much about me. I'm getting better every day. I know the difference between being tired and being depressed and believe me, I'm just tired. I'd tell you if it were otherwise. Now go to dinner and have a nice time."

Kara smiled as she closed the screen door behind her and walked around the veranda to the front of the house. Craig was sitting on the steps smoking a cigarette and gazing out over the plain. "Hi," she said, sitting next to him.

"Hi, yourself." He eyed her outfit. "You're going to get your slacks dirty sitting there."

"I don't mind." She leaned her back against the railing post and looked out at what seemed to be an endless horizon line. Suddenly two gazelle-like creatures bounded past as though their feet were attached to springs that sent them flying straight into the air. It was comical. "What on earth are those?" she asked in laughing amazement.

"Springbok."

"What a perfect name."

They bounced in a circle and went past them again. Kara watched in fascination, trying to figure out how in the world they did it.

"A lot of animals have come to realize that they're safe here," Craig explained. "The compound and the land surrounding it has become something of a haven for them."

"So I gathered. I met one of your snakes earlier. We showered together."

Craig grinned. "Lucky snake. Julius?"

"That's the one."

"He's always had an eye for the ladies. Hope he didn't scare you too badly."

"No comment."

His grin grew wider.

Kara wrapped her arms around her knees. She could hear monkeys chattering but she couldn't see them. "How long have you lived out here?"

"It seems like forever at times. In reality, Lucas and I came out here about ten years ago."

"Why here? Why the Serengeti?"

"Because it's an incredible place. And because the government agreed to let us have free run of the territory to work with the animals and environment any way we see fit."

"Are you a doctor, too?"

He took a long drag off his cigarette. "No. I never had the discipline to apply myself in school. Lucas does the doctoring. I help where I can with the animals, of course, but mostly I do the fund-raising."

"It must take a lot of money to keep a place like this operating."

Craig shrugged. "We make do as best we can with whatever's available. Frankly, we never have enough money. Things break and we can't afford to get them fixed. The helicopter is a prime example. It's been a tremendous help to us in tracking animals, but it has a lot of downtime. It's been out of commission for the past two months." He looked at her sideways. "I don't suppose you're stinking rich with thousands of dollars you've just been aching to donate to a game reserve?" he asked, only half joking.

Kara laughed, but then grew more serious. She did have money and she could help.

Silence fell between them for a time.

"Do you ever get lonely way out here?" Kara asked.

"Oh, sure. And when it gets to be too much for me, I fly myself to the city for a few days."

"What about Lucas?" She didn't want to care about what the man did, but she couldn't help asking the question.

"Are you kidding? He thrives on the solitude out here."

"Somehow that doesn't surprise me."

"Oh, yeah. Association with others is at the bottom of his list of life's necessities."

"Particularly those of the female persuasion, no doubt."

Craig grinned at her. "I see the two of you have met."

"Under less-than-ideal circumstances, I'm afraid. I can only imagine what a stunning first, second and third impression I made on him."

"Don't worry abut it. Once he gets used to having you and your sister around, he'll warm up a bit."

"Just a bit?"

"Never more than that." He looked at her more closely. "Don't expect anything other than civility out of him. You'll be disappointed."

"Believe me, at this point civility from that man would almost seem like a proposal of marriage."

His grin grew wider. "He must really have given you a hard time."

Kara leaned her chin on her knee. "You seem to have maintained your equilibrium well enough."

"Oh, don't let this carefree exterior fool you. I get angry, too. I just have a hard time keeping it at full pitch when it involves a couple of very attractive women." He wiggled his eyebrows at her. "And speaking of women," Craig said as he looked over his shoulder. "Where's that lovely sister of yours?"

"Resting. It's been a long day for her."

"But she'll be out for dinner, right?"

"She says not."

"Well, we'll see about that." He stood up. "I've been looking forward to having dinner with the two of you all day long. She's not going to disappoint me now. Excuse me."

Kara watched with interest as he disappeared around the corner. This kind of attention was exactly what Quinn needed.

She rose with a sigh and looked around. There was a large outcropping of rocks about a hundred yards away. It seemed a perfect place to watch a sunset, and that's what Kara decided to do.

She'd walked perhaps thirty feet when she sensed something behind her. She stopped and slowly turned.

The cheetah stopped also and warily eyed Kara.

Kara stared back. "You again," she said. "I don't suppose you'd know what I meant if I said 'heel'?"

The big cat just stared at her.

"I didn't think so." She turned, again slowly, and started walking, expecting at any moment to find herself facedown on the ground. She could feel the cheetah following her.

Kara continued walking as she glanced over her shoulder. Sophia had kept the same distance between them. Maybe she wasn't going to jump her after all.

When she got there, Kara stood at the base, her hands on her hips, and eyed the outcropping. It was a little more daunting close-up than it had been from the veranda—not because it was particularly high, but because the stones were so large and so smooth. She spotted what looked like a reasonable foothold, took a deep breath and started climbing.

She'd made it up about seven feet, and was getting increasingly pleased with herself. The stepladder in her kitchen was the last mountaineering effort she'd made. She was perhaps a little cocky, but it didn't last long. Her foot slipped and she lost her balance. Her knee banged painfully into a rock and she scraped her hands as she grasped at the rocks to catch herself. The stepladder hadn't really prepared her for anything like this.

When she regained her footing, she stopped for a moment to catch her breath, then started back up. Finally she reached the top. It was only ten or twelve feet from the ground, but she felt as though she'd climbed Mount Everest. She didn't spend a lot of time contemplating what that said about the condition she was in. She, to whom any physical exercise was anathema.

Out of breath, she gratefully sat on the edge of a sun-warmed flat stone, gazing out at the plain. The cheetah settled onto the rock beside her, watching.

Kara turned her head. Their eyes met. She suddenly realized that she wasn't afraid of the cheetah. There was nothing threatening in Sophia's manner. It was as though she was trying to size up Kara before she decided whether or not to befriend her. Kara found that to be very reasonable behavior.

She took a deep breath of the evening air. There was a scent to it like nothing she'd ever experienced. Different even from that afternoon. It was like simple, good clean earth.

And the sounds. They were all around her, filling the sky and washing over her. Crossing her legs, Kara rested her hands on her knees, raised her face to the sky and closed her eyes.

Lucas came around the corner of the house, his hair still damp from the shower. He'd changed into clean, faded blue jeans and a striped shirt. As he looked out at his favorite view in the world, he saw Kara, and unconsciously stopped to watch her.

She was completely still. Lucas had never seen a human being that still. The cheetah was still as well, sitting on its haunches, watching Kara.

After a few minutes, Sophia moved closer to Kara and stretched her lithe body out beside her, luxuriating in the residual warmth of the stone as the evening air grew progressively cooler.

Kara sensed the movement. Opening her eyes, she looked down at the cat and smiled, but didn't touch her.

No one was more surprised than Lucas at what he was seeing. Pleasantly surprised. He walked with his long-legged stride to the rocks and stood beside them, his arms folded across his chest, his shoulder leaning against the gray stone. "Have you ever seen an African sunset?" he asked without looking up at her.

Kara shook her head. "No," she said in a whisper, not wanting to disturb the exquisite stillness surrounding her.

The sky was just beginning to turn a fiery red. "They're spectacular, but they don't last very long. Enjoy it while you can."

Kara wondered why he was being so nice all of a sudden, but didn't question it. She just absorbed the colors in the sky, pulling them into her soul and holding them quietly there for as long as she could.

Lucas looked up at her profile. Her face was lovely; completely open. It was a face that was incapable of keeping secrets or hiding feelings.

He watched her until the sunset faded and night began to fall. Kara looked down at him, her eyes alight. "It's incredible. This whole place is incredible. It's like an exquisite cathedral."

Lucas's expression remained inscrutable, even as his eyes met hers, but she didn't give up. She'd made contact with him and she didn't want to lose it.

"I can see why you love it here so much."

Lucas lowered his gaze and stared out at the horizon. "From the moment I first saw this place, it became my home."

"I can imagine."

"What can you imagine?" he asked, sure that she couldn't imagine at all.

"That this place can seep inside you until it becomes your very life's blood. The sounds, the smells, the colors. I know I've only been here for a few hours, but I'll never look at the world in quite the same way again."

Lucas cocked an eyebrow. "I'm impressed."

Kara didn't try to hide her amusement. It sparkled in her eyes, charming the man despite himself. "Why? Because I'm not as shallow as you thought?"

"Something like that," he agreed amiably.

Her smile grew. "Why are you being nice all of a sudden?"

"I wouldn't call it nice. I'm merely being civil."

"You call it what you want, I'll call it what I want. The big question on the table is 'why?'"

"Don't worry about it." A corner of his mouth lifted in the barest hint of a smile. "It'll pass."

"Oh, great."

"Besides, whether I like it or not, you're here. There's no sense in making things more unpleasant than they absolutely have to be."

Kara put her hand dramatically over her heart. "Oh, please, you'll turn my head." She grew thoughtful. "Have you ever considered a career in the greeting-card business?"

Lucas glanced up at her expressionlessly.

"You're a tough audience," she told him.

This time he almost smiled a real smile—but not quite.

The cheetah rose, once more stretched its long body and ambled down the rocks, not bothering to look back as she headed across the plain.

"Where's she going?" Kara asked.

"Sophia doesn't think you're funny, either."

Kara threw him a look. "Seriously."

His eyes followed the cat. "Seriously, it's her dinnertime."

"So, even though she's your pet, she still hunts?"

"That's right." He looked at his watch. "It's our dinnertime, too. Let's go back to the house."

Kara looked behind her, trying to decide whether she'd be better off climbing down the back or sliding down the smooth face her legs were dangling over. It was only about a twelve-foot drop.

"Drop down," Lucas said, reading her thoughts.

Kara looked at the ground. "I don't know. I'm not known for landing on my feet."

"I'll catch you."

She looked at him suspiciously.

"Trust me."

Kara didn't give it another thought. She simply pushed herself off the rock and Lucas, true to his word, caught her firmly with his large hands at her waist and lowered her to the ground.

Kara put her hands on his shoulders and looked up at him. She wanted to say thank-you or something, but the words stuck in her throat. He was so close to her. He smelled so good. His shoulders were hard beneath her soft hands. And his eyes were looking straight into hers. She could feel her heart pounding faster and faster.

"Are you all right?" he asked, looking at her curiously.

"Fine. Just fine." It came out breathier than she wanted. "Thank you for catching me, Lucas." That sounded a little better. A little more in control.

He was still looking at her strangely.

Kara's hands fell to her sides. She'd never had such a primal reaction to a man's touch. She wasn't sure she liked it.

And yet she liked it very much.

Kara was quiet as they walked toward the house, glancing at Lucas every few moments, not wanting to get caught gawking at him like a teenager with overactive glands. She'd always analyzed feelings—hers and everyone else's. She prided herself in being able to separate herself from a situation, and being able to see it clearly for what it was. This was no different. She found Lucas so attractive because there was something as untamed about him as the animals he cherished. Intellectually she knew he was trouble and she'd do well to keep her distance. But intellect had nothing to do with her body's elemental response to his nearness.

When they got to the porch, Craig was sitting on the steps, dejected and alone.

"What happened?" Kara asked sympathetically.

"Your sister's a tough sell. I gave it my best shot, but I couldn't get her to come to dinner."

Kara sat next to him and patted his knee. "Don't take it so hard. She really is tired. Tomorrow will be different."

"I don't think you quite understand what a blow this is," he said gloomily. "My charm has never let me down this badly."

"What are you talking about?" Lucas asked.

"Her sister," Craig said, inclining his head toward Kara. "She doesn't want to join us for dinner."

"Where is she?"

"In her room, but..."

Lucas didn't wait for Craig's protest. He just left the two of them behind and headed for Quinn's room.

"If I can't get her out, I don't know what makes him think he can," Craig said.

Kara didn't say anything as she rubbed her hands up and down her cold arms. She had her own thoughts about Lucas to deal with at the moment.

"You look chilly," Craig said. "Let's go inside."

Joe was already in the well-lighted game room, standing at a small bar along the far wall. He beamed cheerfully at Kara. "What can I get for you?"

She started to ask for a mineral water, but decided she wanted something a little stronger. "A dry sherry, please."

"Sorry. That's a little too civilized for us."

"What do you have?"

He looked at the various bottles. "Scotch, Irish whiskey, more scotch, beer, more scotch, more beer, soda, orange juice, tea, lemonade and water."

"Orange juice, please."

"One orange juice, coming up. What about you, Craig?"

"Whiskey, neat."

Hilda, her husband in tow, strode firmly into the room. "See, Bertie? I told you we weren't late."

Kara had just sat on the couch.

"Would you mind moving to a chair so that Bertie and I can sit together here?" Hilda asked, towering over her.

"Of course not." Kara rose and moved to a chair across from the couch.

"Here you go." Joe handed her a glass of orange juice.

"Thanks."

He winked at her and turned to the couple. "What can I get for the two of you?"

"I'd like a scotch," Bertie said.

His wife looked at him with a frown. "Don't be ridiculous, Bertie. We'll both have tea." She took a quick look around the room. "I trust that Dr. Pierson will be joining us for dinner?"

Craig perched on the arm of Kara's chair. "He'll be here any minute."

"Do you happen to know what our schedule is for tomorrow?"

"That'll be up to Lucas."

"I don't think so," Hilda informed him. "For the money we're paying for the privilege of staying in this awful place, we intend to have substantial input into what we do while we're here. Isn't that right, Bertie?"

Bertie had picked up a magazine from the coffee table and was already engrossed in an article. "Yes, dear."

Kara heard footsteps on the veranda and looked up just as Lucas came through the door. His gaze went straight to her and locked on her face.

The conversation surrounding Kara turned into dim background noise. Craig spoke to her, but she didn't hear him. She wasn't aware of anyone or anything but the man in front of her.

She finally remembered to breathe.

Craig shook her arm.

Kara looked at him blankly. "What?"

"I told you to look who's here."

She looked back at Lucas.

Craig put his hand on top of her head and turned it slightly to the right. "There."

"Quinn!" she exclaimed as she rose and walked toward her sister. "I'm so glad you came!"

"Lucas convinced me," she said with a smile.

Kara looked at Lucas, suddenly—and unnaturally—shy. "Thank you."

He looked at her for a long moment but didn't say anything. "Quinn," he said, his eyes still on Kara, "would you like something to drink?"

"What are you drinking, Kara?" she asked.

Kara looked blankly at her glass. "It's . . . it's . . ."

"Orange juice," Craig finished for her.

"That sounds good. I think I'll have that."

Quinn sat in a chair beside Kara while Lucas went to the bar. Kara watched as he poured the juice and brought it to her sister.

"Thank you, Lucas," Quinn said, smiling up at him.

He smiled back.

Kara couldn't believe her eyes! The man had actually smiled!

"I want to speak with you," Hilda said authoritatively. "We have the matter of our itinerary to clear up."

Lucas sat in a chair on the other side of the couch and stretched his long legs out in front of him. "I have everything arranged. For the first week the four of you will be leaving here on day-long safaris."

"Meaning what?" Hilda asked.

"Meaning that you'll return here each evening. The second week you'll be going farther afield and spending several days camping out, tracking the animals. The third week, you'll tell us what you want to do and we'll do our best to accommodate you." He looked at

Hilda and Bertie. "I trust that meets with your approval?"

Hilda nodded. Bertie looked at Hilda and nodded.

"Good."

"Lucas," Joe said from across the room, "do you want something to drink?"

"No. I'm going back out tonight."

"What can you do at night?" Kara asked.

"Check on some animals who aren't out during the day." He got a distinctly challenging look in his blue eyes. "Want to come with me?"

"I'm sure I'd just be in the way."

"Well, if you don't feel you're up to it..."

Kara unconsciously sat straighter. "I didn't say I wasn't up to it."

"So you're coming?"

This was a direct challenge. He thought she was good for nothing. He thought she couldn't handle it. "Sure," she said with an attempt at nonchalance. "I'll come. Why not?"

"Why not, indeed."

Craig and Joe exchanged surprised looks. Lucas never invited any of Saragi's guests on his outings.

"You'll need to change your clothes for some that are sturdier and a little warmer," Lucas told her.

"All right."

He looked from Kara to Quinn. "Would you like to come, Quinn?"

"Oh, no. To tell you the truth, I'm not thrilled about being here during the day. The night is going to take a little more getting used to."

"Then maybe I should stay here, too," Kara said, trying not to sound too much like she was looking for a way out.

"Don't be silly," Craig said. "We'll take good care of her. Besides, I'm a lot better company than Lucas, as I'm sure you'll discover on your own."

Lucas just smiled.

A woman Kara hadn't seen before came into the room and said something in a language Kara didn't understand. Lucas answered her, and apparently said something amusing because she gave him a huge smile. "Shakira," Lucas said in English, "these are our guests, Miss Stanhope, Mrs. Whitcomb and Mr. and Mrs. Griffin. Everyone, this is Shakira. She's the wife of Ajani, one of our best deputy rangers, and she takes care of us."

The tall woman inclined her head toward all of the newcomers and then quietly returned to wherever she'd come from. Joe followed her, and a moment later came out with plates of food that he put on the table.

"Can I help?" Kara asked, rising.

"No, thanks," Joe said. "I almost have it." He made two more trips as they all sat at the serviceable round wood table. Quinn sat with Lucas on one side and Craig on the other. Kara was between Craig and Joe, almost directly across from Lucas. Hilda and Bertie were on Joe's other side.

"Isn't Shakira going to join us?" Kara asked.

Lucas shook his head. "She and her husband are Masai. They live with other members of their tribe in their own village not too far from here. She's already on her way home."

Kara looked over the dinner. It was pretty ordinary fare: lamb, potatoes and a canned vegetable. Nothing exotic like snake or gazelle, she was pleased to see.

Quinn picked at her meal, pushing the vegetable around her plate instead of eating it. Craig noticed. "I'm sorry about the canned stuff, but getting fresh produce all the way out here before it rots is nearly impossible."

"Getting anything out here while it's still fresh is nearly impossible," Joe added. "But you get used to it. And Shakira's a good cook."

"I think it's delicious," Kara said. And it really was. She couldn't define the spices that had been used, but they added a delicate touch to what otherwise would have been bland food.

"Joe," Lucas said between bites, "I'll need the plane tomorrow."

"No can do."

"Why not?"

"The engine is knocking. It started just before I landed here this afternoon. I think there's a problem with a bearing, and I don't have a replacement part."

"Did you order it?"

"Yeah, but there's no telling when It'll arrive, as you well know."

"Then we'll have to use the Range Rovers and two of the other trucks tomorrow."

"What are you doing tomorrow?" Kara asked.

"We have some animals that need to be moved from one area to another," Lucas said, looking at her.

"How do you do that?"

"Dart them with a tranquilizer gun and transport them in flatbed trucks." He set his fork on his plate. "If you're coming with me, Kara, you'll have to hurry."

She wished there was some graceful way out of this, but there wasn't, so she gulped a couple of quick bites and got up from the table. "I'll change and be right back."

"I'll bring the Range Rover around front and pick you up there."

Kara raced to her room, stripped out of the clothes she was wearing and put on jeans and a white, oversize man's shirt. She'd only brought one sweater and she threw it over her shoulders, tying the sleeves in front as she ran out her door and to the Range Rover—and the man waiting inside.

Chapter Three

"Was that fast enough?" Kara asked breathlessly as she climbed into the vehicle.

Lucas glanced at her as he put the Range Rover into gear. "Are you looking for applause?"

She grinned at him. "Yes."

He shook his head.

The Rover hit a rut and lurched. Kara gripped the dusty dashboard to avoid being thrown against the door. "What was that?" she gasped.

"Get used to it."

The Rover lurched the other way and she flew into his shoulder. "Ssssorry," she said as she tried to right herself in her own seat. "Howww fa-ar-ar-ar-are we go-o-o-ing?" she asked, doing her best to keep her voice level and failing miserably.

"About ten miles."

Lucas didn't seem to be having any trouble talking, she noticed.

The headlights bounced wildly over the landscape even though they couldn't have been going more than fifteen miles an hour.

Kara couldn't believe it. Her muscles quickly grew stiff from the effort of holding on to whatever she could get her hands on that was attached to the Rover. Minutes crawled by. For more than an hour her body took a beating without any relief. When Lucas finally stopped the car, she'd been clutching the door arm so tightly that she couldn't uncurl her fingers for a few moments.

Lucas pulled slowly into some brush and stopped. "Are you all right?" he asked Kara absently as he reached around behind their seat to gather some things.

"Just fine."

"You don't sound sincere."

"You're kidding!"

He straightened and looked at her in the dim overhead light. "This is real life in the Serengeti, Kara. Too tough for you already?"

She didn't say anything.

Lucas looked at her for a moment longer, then climbed out of the car. When Kara didn't get out right away, he looked in through his open window at her. "Are you coming with me or are you going to spend the night in there?"

"I'm coming, I'm coming," she grumbled. It took her a few seconds to find the door handle. Just as she was about to pull on it, Lucas opened her door and held out his hand. "I don't need your help, thank you," she said as she swiveled and put her feet on the ground.

"Yes, you do."

"No, I don't."

She stood up and her legs promptly buckled. Lucas caught her around the waist with one strong arm and pulled her up straight. "Yes, you do," he repeated.

Kara leaned heavily against his side. It was as though the earth was bucking, trying to throw her off. "What happened?"

"Don't worry about it," he said. "You'll get your sea legs in a few days."

"Sea legs?"

"It's rough getting used to this terrain, but you will. Just give it a little time."

She tried to straighten away from him, but Lucas held her close against him. "Just give yourself another minute or two."

She did, aware every moment of the man holding her. "I'm all right now," she finally said, her voice husky.

Lucas took his arm away, but watched her to make sure she was steady on her feet.

She looked up at him in the moonlight. "Thank you."

His eyes met hers. "That's what I'm here for."

"Hardly, but thank you anyway." She looked around at the moonlit brush and rock outcroppings. "What do we do now?"

Lucas, with surprising gentleness, took Kara by the hand and led her to a spot about twenty feet from a nearly dry riverbed. "Just sit here and be quiet."

Kara winced as she sank to the ground and crossed her legs.

Lucas sat beside her. For the first time she noticed that he had camera equipment with him.

The moon reflected off what little water there was.

"Why are we here?" she whispered.

"This is where the night predators come. I try to keep track of them as best I can. The camera is a terrific help."

"How do you know they haven't been here already? How do you know they're not going to another watering hole?"

"Because the nearest watering hole after this one is fifty miles away."

"Oh."

"Shhhhh."

"Sorry."

It was eerie, sitting in the middle of nowhere in the moonlight with unrecognizable noises around them. Insect noises. Howls.

They sat for a long time.

Quite suddenly, from a place not far away, there was a kind of hoarse, repetitive grunting. The air vibrated with it. "What's that?" she whispered as she leaned toward Lucas.

"Lions."

"I see." She was quiet for a few minutes as she listened to the continuing grunting. "I don't mean to be an alarmist but, just out of curiosity, what's to keep the lions from attacking us?"

"Not a thing."

"Fascinating."

Lucas smiled into the darkness. "Lions don't usually attack people."

"They don't usually? Meaning that they do sometimes?"

"Right."

Kara looked nervously over her shoulder. "I hope you're never in a job where you have to comfort someone for a living. I don't think you're promotion material."

"Tell you what. If a lion jumps on you, I'll save you."

"Uh-huh. And what if a lion jumps on you first?" she asked.

"Then you save me."

"I don't think so."

The grunting sounded nearer. It was a strange noise, frightening and sensual at the same time. Kara moved closer to Lucas. As far as she knew, he didn't have a gun with him, but he made her feel safer.

He looked down at the top of her head in the moonlight. "Were you a tomboy when you were younger?" he asked conversationally, "Or more on the prissy side?"

"I liked to play baseball and climb trees, so I guess you'd say I was a tomboy."

"Good. I like that in a woman."

She looked around, trying to figure out exactly where the lions were. "How about fear? Do you like that in a woman?"

"Depends on the circumstances."

"I'd say that these seem like pretty good circumstances."

She could feel him smiling. "Kara, nothing's going to hurt you."

She took a deep breath and slowly exhaled. Her shoulder was against Lucas's. That connection was the only thing that kept her calm. Or, at least, relatively calm.

The grunting stopped as suddenly as it had begun.

Kara inhaled sharply. The silence was worse than the grunting. At least when the lions were grunting, she could tell where they were. "Why did they stop?"

"Maybe they ran out of things to talk about."

"Don't develop a sense of humor now. I want you to be your mean and nasty self for when the lions come."

"Sorry. I lost my head."

The minutes ticked by. Kara was in a constant state of alert. Lucas was looking through his telephoto lens toward the watering hole as nonchalantly as if he were waiting for a trusted friend.

Kara grew progressively uneasy. She felt as though she was being watched. "Something's out there," she whispered to Lucas as she looked around, her eyes straining to pierce the darkness.

"Lots of things are out there, Kara."

She narrowed her eyes, looking harder. Two gold spots shone back at her like reflectors.

She looked more closely and suddenly there were two more.

And two more. What on earth?

They blinked.

She inhaled sharply and grasped Lucas's arm. "I was right! Something's looking at us! Do you see those gold spots? They just blinked."

"Those are the lions," he said, completely unruffled. "We seem to be in the middle of a pride."

"A pride?"

"A group. A family."

Her heart sank. "Oh, my."

"You don't have anything to worry about. They've made their kill for the evening. Now they're coming here to drink and clean up."

Kara latched on to what little comfort his words offered. "So what you're saying is that they've probably already had dinner."

"Exactly."

"Meaning that they aren't hungry any longer," she said, more to herself than to the man beside her. "That's good. That's very good."

"You talk too much."

"Sorry."

"Don't be sorry. Just be quiet."

"Right." Kara took her hand from his arm and sat quietly staring out at those gold eyes.

The minutes ticked by silently. There was a rustling in the brush and the gold eyes began to move. The lions came out of the brush and headed for the water. The moonlight glinted off their fur. They were surprisingly visible once they came out of the brush. They turned their backs on the humans they knew were there as though they had no fear for their safety.

When they did that, Kara stopped being afraid as well, though it took her a few minutes to realize it.

Her body slowly began to relax. Her heart rate went down. As she watched these beautiful animals behaving as naturally as though there were no people around, a wonderful sensation of belonging—of being one with the animals she was watching—filled her with a quiet joy. She'd never experienced anything remotely like it.

Lucas's camera quietly clicked and whirred.

Kara saw seven lions and three cubs drinking at the water hole. For the first time, though, Kara noticed that one female lion stood slightly away from the group and continued to watch Lucas and her.

The lioness took a few steps toward them and stopped about fifteen feet away. She raised her head and sniffed the air. After perhaps a minute, the lioness came even closer and stopped perhaps ten feet away.

When she moved forward again and came to within three feet of Kara, the newfound sense of peace developing within Kara evaporated as quickly as it had appeared. The lioness stopped and stared at her.

Kara held her breath, but the pounding of her own heart thundered in her ears. The lioness had no interest in Lucas. It was as though she already knew and trusted him—but didn't know what to make of Kara yet.

Kara willed herself to not be afraid; willed herself to not move or breathe. She averted her eyes from the animal's so she wouldn't be perceived as challenging the big cat.

After an eternity, or so it seemed to Kara, the lioness turned and walked away, back to the water hole. This time she drank her fill and joined the rest of the pride as they left the area.

Kara put her hand over her heart and fell back onto the brown grass.

Lucas looked down at her and grinned. His teeth were white in the moonlight. "I'm proud of you. You did very well. Your instincts are good."

Kara aimed her gaze at the Australian. "I could have been killed."

"But you weren't."

"No thanks to you. You just sat there while that lioness looked at me like I had 'dessert' printed across my forehead."

"Do you often get looked at like you're dessert?" he asked, seemingly amused.

Kara didn't want to smile, but she couldn't stop the slight curving of her mouth. "Not quite that literally. And never by lions." She looked up at him in the moonlight. "Well, Dr. Lucas Pierson, what other exciting, life-threatening adventures do you have in store for me tonight?"

"Bored already?"

"Not bored. Certainly not bored. I'm beginning to think that having a pounding heart is a natural state out here."

"A little fear is good to have. You should never take anything for granted out here. You'll live a lot longer."

Kara, suddenly uncomfortable in her prone position with this man looking down at her, sat up. She took her sweater from around her shoulders and slipped her arms into it, more for something to do to cover her uneasiness than anything else. "It's really cold."

"You'll get used to it."

Kara glanced at him out of the corner of her eye. Lucas was rugged looking even in the moonlight. She found that ruggedness very appealing. But even more appealing to her was the unexpected gentleness she sensed in him.

There was a rustling in the brush.

Kara held her breath and listened closely. Were the lions back?

A moment later she saw a trio of the strangest, scruffiest looking dogs, all looking malnourished and in need of a bath. Their ears were huge.

Kara started to ask Lucas what they were, but as though sensing that she was about to speak, he clasped his hand around her arm. Lucas watched the three dogs, but seemed to be waiting for something.

She could feel his tension and it made her more alert. "What's wrong?" Kara whispered.

"I've been following these dogs for the past two years. A female and her two pups are missing."

"Maybe she'll be along later."

Lucas shook his head. "Something must have happened to them."

He really seemed concerned. "Is there something special about them?" Kara asked.

"They're very rare. Nearly extinct. They've been killed off until there are only a few hundred of them left. Anytime another one dies, it impacts the entire population. One less producer of pups." He watched the dogs drinking. "Damn," he said softly.

"We could look for them," Kara suggested.

"The odds of our finding them are slim to none."

"But we can still try."

Lucas grew thoughtful. "I tracked them to their home a few months ago," he said more to himself than to her. "We should probably start there, if I can find it in the dark."

"Then let's do it."

Lucas looked at her for a long minute and nodded. "All right. Come on."

He gathered up his camera equipment and together they walked to the Range Rover. Without saying anything, he started the engine, turned on the headlights and pulled out.

They'd driven for perhaps twenty minutes—twenty long bone-cracking minutes—when Kara spoke for the first time. "Where do they live?"

"They used to live on a kopje a bit south of here."

"A kopje?"

"One of those outcroppings of rocks that you sat on tonight to watch the sunset."

"Oh."

"Whether or not they're still living there is anyone's guess. And if something happened to the mother, the chances of the pups surviving are very poor."

Kara strained her eyes, trying to pierce the darkness on the sides of the Rover where the headlights didn't penetrate. Lucas would occasionally stop the car, turn on the bright spotlights attached to the roof of the car and turn them 360 degrees. Kara saw all kinds of fascinating creatures looking back at them, but no wild dogs.

It was nearly an hour and a half later when the Rover's headlights picked out yet another kopje. "This is it!" Lucas said, recognizing it. He stopped the Rover near the rocks and hit the horn for several short and one long burst. Animals the lights hadn't picked out scattered.

"Why did you do that?" Kara asked, thinking it was rather mean of him.

"I don't want to have to fight with the other animals over whether or not I can search for the pups." He got out of the Range Rover and aimed the spots at the rocks, sweeping the beams back and forth. Nothing moved.

Kara climbed out of the Rover and stood with her arms resting on the open window, her eyes following the light. "What do you think?" she asked.

"I don't think anything yet."

She waited patiently, continuing to follow the light.

"Kara," Lucas said as he reached into the Rover for a flashlight, "you stay near the truck. I'm going to get a closer look."

"Why can't I come with you?"

"Because I don't know what's there."

Kara watched as he approached the rocks, playing the beam of his large flashlight over them. She felt the tension growing inside her, afraid that something was suddenly going to leap at Lucas out of the darkness.

He climbed up the rocks, peering into all of the nooks and crannies, painstakingly examining every inch of the large outcropping. "I've got something," he finally shouted from behind the rocks.

Kara ran toward his voice and found him crouched on the ground, his flashlight next to him, shining into a small cubby. Kara knelt beside him. "What is it?" she asked.

"A pup," he said, lifting a small furry body out of the hole.

"Is it alive?" she asked. It was so still.

"Barely. The other one didn't make it."

Kara peered into the hole and saw a dead puppy. Her eyes stung with sudden tears. "Oh, no," she breathed. "What happened?"

"I'm sure it either starved or dehydrated."

"So their mother is dead?"

"I'm afraid so. Nothing short of that would have kept her from her pups." He handed Kara the puppy that was still alive. While she cuddled it against her breast, Lucas removed his shirt and handed that to her, as well. "Wrap it up so it stays warm."

Kara laid the shirt on the ground and gently set the puppy on it, wrapping it securely. The little thing gazed at her with such sad, tired eyes. "You'll be all right," she said softly, as though the puppy could understand her. "We'll take care of you." She picked the puppy up again and held it against her as she followed Lucas to the Rover.

"Go ahead and get in," he told her as he opened the back door to get something.

Kara sat down, still holding the animal against her.

Lucas came back with a bottle of water. Forming a bowl with the palm of his left hand, he poured some water in it, then dipped his fingers into it and held them up to the puppy's mouth. The puppy looked at him but didn't respond. He dipped his fingers again and gently rubbed them against the puppy's mouth. Again, it didn't react.

Lucas sighed. "Look," he said to Kara, "the puppy is dehydrated as well as hungry. It needs water. You try to get it to take some while I drive us back to Saragi."

"All right."

He anchored the bottle beside her and closed the door. Kara lay the puppy on her lap, still wrapped warmly in Lucas's shirt, and did the same thing with the water that Lucas had, dabbing it against the puppy's mouth one wet fingertip at a time. "Come on, baby," she coaxed. "You can do it. Just one lick."

The puppy just lay there looking at her.

Lucas put the Rover into gear and headed back to Saragi. It was every bit as bumpy as it had been earlier, but Kara balanced herself a little better. The puppy was getting jarred too much on her lap, so she picked it up and cradled it in the crook of her arm while dipping her finger into the water bottle and trying to entice the puppy by touching it to its mouth. It wasn't responding, but Kara did it again and again, determined.

And then the puppy gave her a tiny lick.

"It took some water!" Kara said excitedly.

"Good. Keep it up."

Kara raised the puppy to her face and rubbed her cheek against its fuzzy little head. "Good, baby," she said softly. "Let's try it again."

The puppy weakly licked at her finger and tried to take it into her mouth to suck on. Kara couldn't remember the last time anything had made her feel so wonderful. She forgot about the bumps and the discomfort. All that mattered was this little life.

When they got to the house, Lucas brought the Rover to an abrupt stop and climbed out. He walked quickly around to Kara's side and opened her door. "Come on," he said impatiently.

She followed him inside. They went straight to the kitchen. Lucas pulled out a pan, put it on the stove and poured a small amount of milk into it. While it was warming, he took a baby bottle from one of the cabinets, rinsed it in hot water and poured the warmed milk into it.

"Here," he said as he handed it to Kara. "She's used to you. Give it a try."

Kara unwrapped the furry little body. The puppy didn't try to stand. It didn't do anything but look at her. She gently touched the nipple to its mouth. It had gotten used to her finger so it licked the nipple and gradually took it into its mouth and started sucking.

Lucas hunkered down next to them. He gently rubbed the puppy's head and moved his fingers over the tiny body.

Kara watched his face as he worked. She saw the gentleness she'd suspected was there beneath the surface.

"It's a girl," he said after a moment.

"Is she going to be all right?" Kara asked.

Lucas straightened and shook his head. "I don't know, Kara. The fact that she's taking some nourishment is a good sign. Whether or not we found her soon enough, only time will tell."

"How much time?"

"We should know by morning." He put his hand over hers and pulled the bottle from the puppy's mouth. "Stop for a few minutes, then give her a little more."

As Kara looked up at him, their eyes met and held.

Lucas was the first to look away. "You should be getting to bed. I'll stay up with the puppy. It's going to need to be fed about every thirty minutes through the night."

"May I help?"

His gaze returned to her face and moved slowly over her features. "You won't get any sleep, Kara."

"That's all right. I don't mind."

Lucas thought about it for a moment, then rose, went to another cabinet and pulled out a hot-water bottle. "We're going to need this," he said as he filled it with hot water from the tap and handed it to her. "And this." He took a one-hour timer from the stove. "I'll get an extra blanket for the puppy to sleep on and meet you in the game room."

While he left the kitchen, Kara went into the game room and turned on a dim corner light with one hand while she held the pup and the water bottle close to her with the other.

She sank tiredly onto the couch and waited for Lucas. He came a minute later. "Here," he said as he draped a blanket around her shoulders. "I thought you might be needing this."

Kara looked up at him, surprised by his thoughtfulness. "Thank you."

He took another blanket, already folded, and set it in her lap as a bed for the puppy and the hot water bottle.

"I know you can't be sure, but in your opinion, is she going to make it?"

"I have a feeling she's going to do just fine."

Kara looked down at the little sleeping face as she lay the pup in the cozy blanket nest.

"Have you ever worked around animals before?" Lucas asked as he sat in a chair across from her.

"No. I've always lived in the city."

"That surprises me. You have something of a knack."

Kara's eyes lit with a smile. "A compliment! How completely unexpected."

"Oh, I'm a master of the unexpected."

Their eyes met and held. "I'm sure you are."

Lucas's eyes rested on her face. He'd been so sure about the kind of person she was going to be before meeting her. Now he didn't know what to think.

The timer sounded.

Lucas rose and went to the kitchen. Kara sat quietly, stroking the pup with her long fingers, talking softly.

He returned a minute later with some warm milk. Kara bumped the nipple against the puppy's mouth. It wiggled a little—something it hadn't done before—and started sucking.

"You sweet thing," she whispered. "You're going to be fine. I'll see to it."

"Don't let it drink too much," Lucas said, watching.

Kara nodded and took the bottle away from the pup while Lucas reset the timer.

Kara leaned her head back against the couch and gazed at the man across from her. "It's going to be a long night," she said tiredly.

A corner of his mouth lifted as he watched her. "Welcome to the Serengeti, Kara."

Chapter Four

Lucas had gone to his small office just off the animal compound to get some files that needed paperwork done. When he got back to the game room, Kara was feeding the wild pup again. She smiled tiredly up at him. "I think you're right about her making it," she said quietly. "Every time she eats, she seems to get a little stronger."

He set his files on the coffee table and looked down at her. "And you get more tired. It's nearly dawn. Why don't you let me finish out the night so you can go to your room and get some sleep?"

"I'm fine. Thanks anyway." She set the bottle on the couch beside her and snuggled the sleepy pup against her breast. "How old is she?"

Lucas sat in his chair and picked up a file. "Five weeks."

"When will she need solid food?"

"As soon as she gets stronger. Perhaps in another week or so, we'll introduce a little ground meat into her diet. Her mother was probably already doing that."

Kara lowered the pup onto the blanket and watched her sleep. "It must be very difficult for you when you find animals you can't save."

"It is."

Kara leaned her head against the back of the couch. "Do you ever get hardened to it?"

Lucas thought for a moment. "I wouldn't call it hardened, but after a while, in addition to the heartbreak, there's anger, particularly when the death of some of these animals involves deliberate destruction. Sometimes I think it's that anger that keeps me going."

They looked at each other.

"I like you," Kara said suddenly. "I didn't think I was going to, but I do."

"Don't like me too much," Lucas said softly.

"I don't expect you'll let me."

The screen door was open. The insect noises from outside were the only noise. Without her really being aware of it, Kara's eyes drifted closed. When she did realize that her eyes were closed, she told herself that she was just going to rest them for a moment. Just a short moment.

Within seconds she was asleep.

Lucas watched her. There was something about her he found very appealing. It occurred to him that he should keep his distance, but he didn't really foresee any problems. She'd be gone in a few weeks and life would return to normal. He knew where his priorities were and he'd never had trouble keeping himself focused on them.

This was no place for a woman to live. And it was the only place he could ever live.

As long as he remembered that, he could just enjoy Kara's company while she was at Saragi and forget about her when she was gone.

Which was not to say that he was going to stop giving her the occasional hard time. She was fun to challenge. And unless he was greatly misreading her, Kara enjoyed being challenged.

Leaning forward, he picked up the timer and turned it off so it wouldn't wake Kara. Then he slipped the puppy from her lap and held it on his own lap for its next feeding....

Kara awoke with a start. When she first opened her eyes, she didn't recognize where she was, but then everything came back to her, including the puppy.

She looked at the empty blanket on her lap. "Oh, no!" She rose so abruptly that the blanket fell to the floor.

"Ah, you're finally awake," Craig said as he crossed the room toward her and handed her a glass of orange juice.

"Where's the pup?"

"Not to worry. Lucas turned it over to the gamekeeper in the compound as soon as he arrived for work this morning. She'll be fine."

Kara leaned back on the couch. "Thank heavens! I was afraid she'd wandered off."

"She's still a little too weak for that."

"So you saw her?" she asked as she took the juice. "How did she look?"

"Wonderful. You and Lucas were lucky to find her so quickly. She would have been dead by now if you hadn't."

"Now that she's here, what will happen to her?" Kara asked as she took a long drink.

"We'll keep her here until she's old enough to take care of herself, then we'll release her into the wild."

"But will she be able to take care of herself? Won't she be too domesticated?"

"That's a danger, of course. We'll have to see when the time comes. A lot of the animals we release feel safe in and around the compound and tend to stay close by. So far it hasn't been a real problem."

"That's good." Kara rubbed her eyes and stretched. "What time is it?"

"About five-thirty."

"Five-thirty?" she groaned. "Are you always up this early?"

"Usually. It's easier to work in the cool of the morning than in the heat of the afternoon."

"I suppose that makes some sort of sense." She yawned and put her hand to her mouth. "Excuse me."

Craig smiled at her. "I've already gotten your sister up. You're going to be leaving on your safari in about an hour, so if you're going to shower you'd better get at it."

"Umm. Craig, about that safari. Do you think it would be all right if Quinn and I went with you guys instead? I mean, a safari sounds really nice, but I'd personally rather watch you at work."

"You're kidding."

"No, I'm not."

"It's hot and dirty."

"I know."

"It can be really boring."

"That's all right."

"I'll have to ask Lucas."

"Okay."

And beside the fact that it was something Kara wanted very much to do, she thought it would be a nice challenge for Quinn. If something like that didn't get her mind off her troubles for a time, nothing would.

"And if he says no," Craig asked, "which he probably will, what then?"

"Then Quinn and I will be good girls and go on the safari with Hilda and Bertie."

Craig nodded. "Let's go ask."

Kara set her juice on the table and followed Craig through the door to the veranda. The sun wasn't quite all of the way up, but already she could feel the cool of the night being slowly burned off. It was going to be another scorcher.

And suddenly there was the strangest sight Kara had ever seen. Lucas, shirtless and in shorts, perspiration beading his bronzed torso, came out of nowhere, running at a pretty good pace, about ten feet in front of a baby rhino who seemed determined to catch up with him. Kara watched in amazement.

"Too late," Craig said. "We'll have to catch him when he gets back."

"Gets back from where?" Kara asked, staring after the odd couple.

Craig laughed. "I see you haven't met Norman yet."

"Norman?"

"Stormin' Norman, our orphaned rhino. He needs to exercise, but about the only way we can get him to do it is to go jogging with Lucas. We discovered it almost by accident when Lucas went running one morning and Norman took off after him. Now the two of them go running together most mornings."

"Now I've seen everything." Kara laughed as she watched the two of them. She couldn't help herself. "I never thought I'd say this about a rhinoceros, but he's cute."

"I know what you mean. And at the moment, he's fairly harmless, but in another year, look out."

"Where did you find him?"

Craig grew more serious. "Wandering the plain. We found what was left of his mother the next day. Poachers."

Kara's eyes filled with quick tears. She'd seen pictures of other rhinos killed for their horns. It didn't take much imagination to know what had happened to Norman's mother. "I don't know if I could ever live out here and do what you do," she said softly. "I think I'd be depressed all of the time."

"It's impossible not to be affected by it," Craig agreed. "I know Lucas is, though you'll probably never hear that from him. He likes to think of himself as an impartial observer and caretaker of nature."

"He's a difficult man to read."

"Don't even try. He doesn't let anyone get close enough to figure him out."

"Why not?"

"Who knows? We've been friends since childhood and I still find myself wondering if I—or anyone—really knows Lucas. He's always been very private." Craig looked at his watch. "You'd better hurry and take your shower. Breakfast is in forty minutes. Be there or go hungry."

Kara went to her room and gathered her things. Not taking any chances when she went into the small bathroom, she checked out the floor thoroughly for any unwanted reptilian visitors, then securely latched the door behind her.

This time she found the shower really pleasant. It was certainly different, but nice.

With her hair still damp, she dressed in cuffed olive shorts, a white T-shirt and sneakers. Gathering up her shower things, she dropped them off in her room and headed out again to Quinn's room. "Hi!" she said cheerfully as she walked in.

Quinn was unpacking. "Hi, yourself," she said with a smile as she took a stack of neatly folded clothes to the dresser. "I understand you had quite a night last night."

"It was really interesting." Kara flopped on her sister's bed and lay back on the pillows, her hands behind her head. "I have a proposal for you."

Quinn looked at her sideways. "Uh-oh."

"I think you'll like it."

"Again, I say uh-oh."

"Instead of going on a safari with Hilda and Bertie, I think we should go on a real trip with Lucas and Craig."

"Gee, I don't know, Kara. I was really looking forward to venturing out day after day—after day—after day with Hilda and Bertie."

Kara grinned at her sister. "So you're game? You'd be willing to do it if Lucas agrees?"

Quinn flashed her sister a dry look. "Let me understand this. My choices are Hilda and Bertie, or Lucas and Craig?"

"Right."

"I'll admit it's tough, but I'd have to go with Lucas and Craig."

"I should warn you that it'll be rough. I went out in the Rover with Lucas last night and I'm covered with bruises from being bounced around."

Quinn smiled. "I can take it. And since we did come all this way, we might as well see the real Africa."

Kara jumped off the bed and hugged her sister. "That's great! This is just what the doctor ordered. I'll see if Lucas is back from his run so I can ask him."

"And if he says no?"

"That was my question. And the answer is a safari with Hilda and Bertie."

Quinn shook her head. "I hate to say it, but almost anything is better than three weeks with Hilda and Bertie."

"Exactly." Kara left Quinn and walked down the veranda to Lucas's room. "Hello?" she called. "Lucas? Are you there?"

He came to the door, his hair wet, a towel around his shoulders. His eyes moved slowly over her face. "Good morning, Kara."

She smiled at him. "Hi. How's the pup?"

"She's fine. She even managed to walk around a bit this morning."

"I'm glad. Sorry I fell asleep."

"It's all right. You'd had a long day."

Kara shifted her weight onto her other foot, trying to figure out how she was going to ask him.

"Is that all?" he said after a moment.

She shook her head.

"Well?"

Kara cleared her throat. "I want you to let Quinn and me go with you today instead of on the safari you've arranged."

Lucas didn't even think about it. "No."

"Why not?"

"You'd just be in the way."

"I wasn't in your way last night, was I?"

"Not really, no."

"So what's the problem?"

"The problem is that I have a job to do and I can't do it as well as I should if I have to keep one eye on you and the other on your sister."

"You won't have to. We can take care of ourselves."

"You don't know anything about taking care of yourself. At least not out here."

"We'll learn as we go along."

"Kara, you're not allowed to make mistakes out here. If you do, you can die. It's that cut-and-dried. The safari I've arranged for you and Quinn is nice and safe."

"And if I don't want nice and safe?"

"Then you came to the wrong place." He looked at his watch. "You'll have to excuse me. Breakfast is in a few minutes and I have to finish getting dressed." Lucas turned away from her, effectively ending their dialogue.

Kara swore under her breath as she walked around the veranda toward the game room. They'd had such a good rapport last night, and now this.

Craig was sitting on one of the tattered veranda chairs. "You look like somebody rained on your parade."

"Lucas," she said, sitting next to him.

"He won't let you go?"

"So he says."

"Don't lose hope yet. Let me give it a try."

Kara looked at him curiously. "Why would you be willing to let us come with you?"

"Purely selfish reasons."

"Which are?"

"I want to have a chance to get to know your sister better. I can't do that if I'm traveling in one direction and she's off in another."

Kara looked at him seriously. "You know she lost her husband about a year ago?"

Craig nodded.

"She's been through a lot."

"I can imagine."

"I want her to get interested in life. Maybe even in men. But I don't want her to get burned in the process. I won't allow it." She looked straight into his eyes. "Do you understand?"

Craig reached over and squeezed Kara's hand. "Yes, I do. And believe me when I say that I would never do anything to risk hurting Quinn. Aside from the fact that you'd nail me, I'm not that kind of man."

Quinn walked around the corner and leaned her hand on the back of Kara's chair. "What are the two of you being so serious about?"

"Life," Kara said with a smile as she looked up at her sister. "It can be a serious business."

"What did Lucas say when you asked if we could go with him?"

"No."

"So I guess it's the wild kingdom with Hilda and Bertie."

Craig rose. "Not necessarily. I'll be back in a minute."

Even as Craig was leaving, men began arriving. Some were in regular shorts and T-shirts, but some were in khaki shorts and shirts that looked like uniforms. They all smiled at Kara and Quinn as they passed, and said good-morning, but didn't stop for conversation.

Craig and Lucas came around the corner together. Lucas looked at Kara, not at all pleased. Craig smiled and winked as they passed and went into the game room.

"What do you suppose that means?" Quinn asked as they followed them inside.

"I think it means that Craig talked him into letting us go and Lucas isn't at all happy about it."

A buffet had been set up. Kara and Quinn got in line behind the others and took some toast and scrambled eggs. Then the two of them went to the couch and sat down to eat and listen as the men discussed their plans for the day.

It was fascinating listening to them talking about what they wanted to accomplish in the time they had, and how they were going to go about doing it. Each man seemed to be in charge of a specific area of the trip, from food to weapons to transportation.

Lucas finished eating quickly and walked over to Kara and Quinn. "Craig seems to think you two should be allowed to go with us."

"And?" Kara asked hopefully.

The muscles in his jaw clenched. "And I'm going to let you. But I expect you to keep up with the rest of us or you'll be right back here."

Kara beamed at him. "Thank you!"

"Don't thank me," he said evenly as his eyes bored into her, already regretting his change of heart. "Just make sure you do everything you're told."

"We will," Quinn and Kara said in unison.

"All right. Let's get out of here."

Craig caught Kara's and Quinn's hands and hurried them out the door. "We have to get you two packed. Do you have any more clothes like what you have on now?"

"Lots," they said, once more in unison.

"Good." He moved them quickly along the veranda, stopping at Quinn's room first. "Do you have anything like a duffel bag?" he asked Kara.

"Just the bags we carried on the plane with us."

"Those will be fine. Kara, while I help Quinn, you go back to your room and pack enough shorts and shirts for a week. Also bring your own soap and towels. Everything'll be crammed in there, but that's fine. No one cares if your clothes are wrinkled.

Kara raced to her room and started pulling things out of the closet and drawers. It was all she could do to get everything in. Just as she managed, with a struggle, to get the zipper closed, Craig hammered on her door. "Come on. Let's go."

Kara ran outside after Craig and Quinn. They found Lucas loading supplies into one of the Rovers. "We're ready," she said breathlessly. "Can I help you with anything?"

"We're all set," he said with a grunt as he shoved the last box inside.

"Which car do you want us in?" Quinn asked.

"Quinn's coming with me," Craig said.

"All right. Kara, you'll be with me," Lucas said.

"But I thought that Quinn and I..."

"I don't have time to stand here arguing with you."

Kara pressed her lips together.

A corner of his mouth lifted. "That's better." He took her shoulder bag and heaved it into the Rover. Then he gave Kara an arm up and heaved her into the Rover. "Let's go."

As soon as he climbed behind the steering wheel, they were off, bumping across the plain in a line of trucks four across. Kara held on for dear life. Dust flew into the air behind them, so thick it obscured their rear view.

Kara was exhilarated. There were long stretches when the ride was almost smooth. During one of them, Kara leaned forward so she could see better, her forearms resting on the dashboard. It was incredible. Even with the dust. She'd never seen so much open space. And the animals! Zebra, digging their hooves into the dirt and galloping away from the noise of the vehicles; giraffes that turned small heads on long necks to watch them go by.

"This is wonderful!" Kara yelled over the whine of the engine. "I can't believe what I'm seeing!"

Lucas looked at her face, alight with enthusiasm. He couldn't help but smile, even as he shook his head.

He reached out suddenly and pressed her back into her seat. "Why'd you do that?" she asked.

At that moment, the Rover hit a hole, flew into the air and came down again. Lucas hardly bothered to slow down.

"Whoa!" Kara said in surprise. "Thank you!"

"No problem. I can't have your chin denting my dashboard. The old thing's in bad enough shape as it is."

Kara laughed.

"Lucas? Lucas? Come in," Craig's voice crackled over a radio. "Do you see the wildebeest to the north?"

Lucas picked up a hand-held radio and pressed a button. "Yeah, I see them."

Even after hearing they were there, Kara couldn't spot them. All she could see was dust.

"Do you want to go through the herd or around it?"

"Around."

"Where are they?" Kara asked, still looking.

"Do you see the dust up ahead?"

"Yes."

"That's the herd. They've obviously been spooked by something. They seem to be running right at us, so we're going to veer a little to the west to avoid them."

"Would they hurt us if we went through them?"

"Themselves more than us. When they run like that, they don't pay any attention to where they're going. They just blindly follow the one in front of them. Thousands of them have been known to run off the edge of cliffs, simply because the ones in front of them did it."

Even as Lucas was speaking, the whole line of vehicles began moving slightly west, away from the approaching cloud of dust. It got very bumpy. Kara was holding on for dear life, and at the same time trying to keep herself still enough to look for the wildebeest. They were several hundred yards away when she was finally able to pick them out of the dust. It was the most incredible thing she'd ever seen. The herd was massive. There were thousands of them, all running. The noise from all those thousands of hooves was deafening. And the vibration! Even through the tires of the bucking Range Rover, she could feel the thunder inside the earth.

Lucas and the other drivers laid on their horns. Kara didn't understand why until she noticed that the herd, in reaction to the sound, headed a little more east, away from them, leaving in their wake a cloud of thick, choking dust.

Kara swiveled in her seat, watching the wildebeest disappearing into the distance. "Do they ever stop?" she asked in amazement.

"They will when they're tired. They came a little early this year."

"Early?"

"They're a migrating animal. They follow the rains. If they're already here, that means the rains must not be far behind."

"Oh!"

They tried to avoid the dust, but they couldn't altogether. There was just too much of it. And it was either suffocate in a closed car or eat the dust.

Kara ate the dust.

Lucas handed her a plastic bottle of water. "Drink some of this."

"Thanks." She unscrewed the cap and held it to her mouth for a few delicate sips.

"Better?" he asked.

"It's like drinking mud," she yelled as she handed him back the bottle. "Too much dust."

"You'll get used to it."

"Oh, good. That's just wonderful." She said it under her breath, but Lucas somehow heard her and smiled to himself as he drank deeply from the bottle.

The ride from hell lasted just under five hours. When Lucas and the others finally stopped, Kara felt as though she was still bouncing in her seat.

Lucas climbed out of the Rover and signaled to Craig to join him. Kara opened her door and gingerly stepped out. Her intention was to walk over to Quinn, but it took her a moment before she was steady enough to cover the ten feet.

Quinn, still in the car, looked at her sister through the window. "You didn't tell me I was going to be crippled for life," she said dryly.

"I forgot about that part." Kara smiled cheerfully at her. "If it's any consolation, I'm told that we'll get used to it."

"Not if I have anything to say about it. After less than twenty-four hours at this place, I think I can safely say that this is going to be my last visit to this—wonderland."

Lucas and Craig walked over to them. "I'm going to be doing some tracking on foot from here. Someone else will drive my car. The rest of you go with Craig to a prearranged spot where camp will be set up."

"I want to go with you," Kara said.

"It's going to be a long, hard walk," Lucas said.

"Anything is better than getting back into that car."

"You won't think so by the end of the day if you go with me."

"I'm willing to risk it."

Lucas thought it over. "You'll have to keep up," he said after a moment, his serious eyes looking into hers. "There'll be absolutely no special consideration because you're either female or a tourist."

"That's fine."

"All right. As long as you understand the ground rules." He walked around to the back of Craig's truck and removed two backpacks. He tossed one of them to Kara, who nearly dropped it because of its unexpected weight.

"What do I do with this?" she asked, looking it over.

"You carry it. It has water, food and a few other things that might come in handy if we can't hook up with the others."

"Why wouldn't we be able to hook up with them?" she asked as she shouldered the pack.

"Things happen." He cocked an eyebrow. "Still want to go, Kara?"

No, she didn't want to go at all. She'd completely changed her mind. "Sure," she heard herself say. "I still want to go."

He took a rifle from the truck and slipped the strap over his shoulder so that it hung down his back. "Then let's do it."

"Just us?" she asked, looking at the others and thinking that there was safety in numbers.

"Just us. We'll have more on foot tomorrow. Right now they're needed to set up camp." Without further ado, he started walking.

Kara looked at her sister, rolled her eyes and followed after him.

The sound of the trucks faded behind them as they walked in an area that the trucks would have been hard-pressed to cover. The terrain was up and down and full of rocks.

Lucas's eyes scanned the ground.

"What are you looking for?" Kara asked.

"Spoor."

"What's that?"

"Tracks. Evidence that someone or something came this way."

Kara began searching also. She saw trampled grass, but she couldn't see any way to tell when it was trampled or by what.

They walked and walked. The heat was incredible. Kara could feel her energy gradually being sapped by it. She switched the backpack from shoulder to shoulder but it kept getting heavier and heavier.

And she kept getting hotter.

Lucas turned to make sure she was keeping up and noticed her flushed cheeks. He didn't say anything, but a few minutes later stopped under the sparse shade of an acacia tree. "Let's rest for a few minutes and have something to drink."

Kara gratefully dropped her pack to the ground and sat unceremoniously on the dirt.

Lucas took a plastic bottle of mineral water from his pack, opened it and held it out to Kara. "Here," he said as he stood over her, "this will help."

She gratefully accepted it and took some sips of the warm water. "Thank you," she said as she handed it back to him.

He watched her as he took a long drink himself. "Aren't you hot with all that hair on your neck?" he asked as he capped the bottle and wiped his mouth with the back of his hand.

"Extremely."

"Do you have anything you can use to tie it back?"

"I didn't even think of it when I was packing."

"We could always cut it off," he suggested.

Kara looked at him for a long moment with narrowed eyes. "You're joking, right?"

He didn't smile as he put the bottle of water back into his pack and took out a long, ugly and lethal-looking knife.

"Right?" she asked again, nervously.

Lucas bent over and cut a handful of long grass. Without saying anything, he flipped the knife into the ground and began braiding the grass.

Kara watched him curiously as his fingers artfully twisted the long strands. When he was finished, he knelt behind her and lifted her thick hair away from her neck.

"You're soaking wet," he said as he trailed a fingertip through the perspiration on the back of her neck.

"I'm hot. I don't think I've ever been so hot."

Lucas gently blew on her neck to cool her off.

Kara closed her eyes. "That feels wonderful. Do it again."

Lucas gazed at the vulnerable line of the back of her neck as she tilted her head forward. Lifting her hair higher, he blew on her neck again, beginning at the hairline and moving down the long line to her shoulder. The gently perfumed scent of her skin and hair drifted to him.

Over him.

Into him.

Kara sighed.

"This should help," he said, suddenly efficient, as he wrapped the braided grass around a ponytail of her hair and tied it.

Kara turned her head and looked at him over her shoulder. "Thank you."

Lucas straightened without responding.

Kara rose also and brushed the dirt off her shorts.

"Are you ready to go on?" he asked.

She nodded.

"You can tell me if you're not. There's no disgrace."

"I'm not a quitter, Lucas."

"Perhaps not under ordinary circumstances, but these are hardly ordinary."

"You said there was to be no special consideration. I agreed to it."

He shrugged. "Have it your way."

Her way, Kara thought. Her way would be to go to a cushy, air-conditioned hotel and sleep for a week. She was exhausted. Nothing in her life had prepared her for this kind of physical exertion. But she was determined to handle it. She'd show him what she was made of. She'd show him.

"Come on."

She focused and found him already twenty feet ahead of her.

Kara took a deep breath, shifted the heavy backpack, and followed him.

Chapter Five

Kara followed along uncomplainingly. Or at least externally uncomplainingly. Had Lucas been able to tap into her thoughts, he would have discovered that her feet were killing her, the bugs were driving her crazy and she'd never been so hot and miserable in her life.

She couldn't stop thinking about the heat. It was really getting to her. It was a suffocating kind of wet heat that made it difficult to breathe—like trying to take in air through a thick blanket. She was sweating so much she could feel it rolling down her face and between her breasts.

She had to stop. If she didn't stop, she was going to die.

Lucas turned to look at her. "Are you all right?"

"Just fine." Kara smiled to punctuate just how really *fine* she was.

"Let's take a break."

"Well, if you feel you absolutely must." Kara stopped right where she was. The backpack hit the ground first. Kara dropped like a rock beside it.

"Are you sure you're all right?" Lucas asked, trying not to show his amusement.

She smiled at him again. "Oh, yes. I'm fine. Just fine."

He pulled out his bottle of water and handed it to her.

"Thank you!" Delicacy was tossed aside as she grabbed the bottle, tilted it straight into her mouth and drank deeply. Water dribbled down her chin, but she didn't care—until she saw Lucas staring at her. She lowered the bottle. Water still dripped down her chin. Kara held out the bottle to him. "I was thirsty," she said sheepishly.

"So I see."

Lucas tilted his head back to drink from the bottle, his blue eyes on the sky as he drank. Kara was mesmerized by the sight of his strong throat muscles moving rhythmically as he swallowed.

He lowered the bottle and his gaze. His eyes locked with hers. As impossible as it seemed, Kara's face flushed even more. And if she'd known how transparent her thoughts were to the man looking at her... But, luckily, she didn't.

Lucas poured water over his fingers as he knelt in front of Kara. Just as she was about to ask him what he was doing, he ran his wet fingertips across her forehead and cheeks, and down her throat. "You look like you're about to have a stroke."

"I'm—"

"I know," he said dryly. "You're fine. Just fine."

She flashed him an ingenuous smile.

For the first time Lucas noticed the faintest hint of a dimple in her right cheek. He leaned back on his heels. "All right, Kara. Tell me how you're really feeling."

"Well, I..."

"The truth."

Kara sighed and looked down at her hands. "The truth is that I'm hot as hell and my feet are killing me."

"Why didn't you tell me that in the first place?"

"Because you were expecting me to get too hot and have murderous feet."

"So?"

"So I didn't want to give you the satisfaction of living down to your expectations. I wanted to show you I was made of stronger stuff."

He tilted her chin so that she was looking at him, spilled some more water onto his fingers and dabbed it on her hot face. "Why?"

"Why what?"

"Why does it matter to you one way or another what I think of you?"

Kara thought about it for a moment and shrugged. "I don't know. It just does."

"It shouldn't. I'm nothing to you but your host. You're nothing to me but a guest visiting my game reserve. And frankly, if I didn't need the money, you wouldn't be here."

Kara flinched. "Ouch."

"It's true." He put the cap back on the water. "Are you hungry? Would you like to eat?"

"What do you have?"

He reached into his pack and pulled out a plastic package. "Dried beef," he said as he opened it and offered her a slice.

She took one. "Thank you."

Lucas took one also and inclined his head.

"What exactly is it that you've been looking at so closely as we've been walking?" Kara asked.

Lucas sat on the ground beside her. "I found some rhino spoor back a mile or so ago. Unfortunately I've also now found human tracks."

"Why unfortunately?"

"It could mean poachers. No legitimate groups have permission to be out here."

Their presence apparently was alarming some birds who started noisily chirping and squawking and beating their wings as they flew from tree to tree.

"What's going on?" Kara asked. She'd heard the noise earlier in their walk, but nothing like this.

"They're telling the animals that danger is near."

She smacked at an insect on her neck. "Sort of a Serengeti early-warning system."

"Exactly."

Kara looked around casually. A little too casually. "Danger, huh? Is there perhaps something—anything—we should be concerned about?"

Lucas grinned at her as he rose. "Come on," he said holding out his hand.

She let him pull her to her feet. "You were probably thinking that question was rhetorical."

He started walking and didn't answer.

"It wasn't," she said, grabbing her backpack and running to catch up with him.

He glanced back at her. "We should always be concerned, but there's no need to be in a constant state of fear. I've been out here for a dozen years and have only been attacked a few times."

"By what?"

"Various animals. But they never sneaked up on me. I knew what was coming before it happened."

She nodded as she looked suspiciously over her shoulder. "Oh, I feel a lot better."

"I'll take care of you, Kara."

She tripped over a tree root hidden from view in the long grass and flew forward. It took her a few steps to catch herself, but she managed to regain her balance before bottoming out.

"Nice save."

"Thanks," she said matter-of-factly, refusing to lose her train of thought. "And what do you mean, you'll take care of me? I thought I was supposed to take care of myself."

"You are. Within reason."

Suddenly they came out of the long grass to a flat, cracked, sun-baked mud stretch of plain. Heat rose from it in visible waves. Kara stopped, her lips softly parted. "What's this?"

"A riverbed. Or at least it is during the rainy season."

"How long has it been dry?"

"For about four months."

"Where do the animals go for water?"

"There's water in the grass and tree leaves. Elephants can dig with their tusks and sometimes find small underground springs. And there's the occasional small water hole, like the one I took you to last night."

A movement across the dry riverbed and to the right caught Kara's attention. She turned her head and saw a giraffe eating leaves from a treetop, its long neck stretching gracefully. There was a young giraffe beside her, its head barely reaching its mother's shoulders. Kara touched Lucas's arm and pointed toward the giraffes. "Why aren't they running away from us?"

"Giraffes don't have much to fear from man and they seem to know it. Besides which, we're downwind."

As they crossed the riverbed and climbed up the bank, she could see that there were gazelles grazing with the giraffes, and a few zebra scattered among them.

Kara touched Lucas's arm to stop him from walking any farther as she watched the animals, afraid he'd disturb them and they'd run away. He started to impatiently shake her off but stopped when he saw her face. His gaze shifted from Kara to the animals, and back to Kara.

He grew still, quite suddenly remembering how he'd felt the first time he'd seen these exotic creatures in the wild with no fences or moats separating him from them. Thrilled. In awe. Vulnerable. He saw all of these emotions chase their way across Kara's open face.

Kara turned her head. Her eyes met his. "For the first time," she said softly, "I think I understand a little of the appeal the Serengeti has for you."

"Don't romanticize this place. That would be a mistake."

"Believe me, that's the last thing I'm doing as I stand here with sweat dripping down my back and swollen, aching feet. But years from now I'll have forgotten how uncomfortable I am and just remember this moment and my first real glimpse of Africa as it should be seen."

"Years from now, all any of us may have of wild Africa may be our memories."

"Things are that desperate?"

He nodded as he looked at the animals who were growing a little restive at the sound of their voices. "Between the toll the poachers are taking and civilization encroaching on the animals' territory, I don't see much of a future for this place."

"And yet you pour all of your energy into it."

"Someone has to. The damage that's already been done can't be undone, but if people pull together and awareness grows, perhaps we can save some of it."

Kara's expression softened. Amazingly, considering what her earlier opinion of the man had been, she found herself admiring him now.

"Come on," Lucas said gruffly, not at all welcoming the change he sensed in her. "We have a lot of territory to cover."

This time she fell into step beside him as they finished climbing the bank and headed toward the animals. The heads of the gazelles shot up as they sniffed the air. The giraffes turned toward them. The zebra grew skittish and bolted. The gazelles followed. The giraffes loped away, but not too far.

Kara did her best to keep up. "It's interesting walking like this," she said, slightly breathless from the fast pace.

"How so?"

"The plain seems so open from the air, but it's really quite deceptive. The grass is long, some of the rock outcroppings are huge and there are lots of small ravines that I didn't notice from the air. It would be easy to hide out here. Is that why you have such trouble finding poachers?"

"Those are considerations, of course. It makes them hard to spot from the air. But mostly it's the sheer size of the area they have to work in. It's impossible to patrol the entire plain. And usually by the time we discover that poachers have been in a certain area, they've already done their damage."

They waded into more grass, setting off a cacophony of sound from the annoyed insects and birds. After an hour, the grass began to get shorter until it was only up around their ankles, and there was a lot of open, dusty soil. Lucas stopped suddenly and bent toward the ground.

Kara leaned over next to him. "What is it?"

"Spoor. Both man and animal have been this way. And not all that long ago. Maybe a day, a day and a half."

"Can you tell what kind of animal?"

"Rhino, I think. It's kind of hard to tell because the human tracks cover the animals tracks." Lucas straightened and started walking again, his eyes on the ground. About a hundred yards away there was evidence of a fire. Lucas poked through it with the toe of his shoe, turning over the charred wood and sifting through the ashes.

"Well?" Kara asked.

"This has been here about as long as the tracks." Lucas kicked at the ashes and swore softly. The corners of his eyes crinkled as he squinted and looked around.

"So what do you do now?"

"We'll follow this for another hour, then break off to go to the campsite for the night." He started following the tracks that only he could see.

Still walking, Lucas pulled the walkie-talkie from his backpack and spoke into it. "Craig? Are you there?"

After a moment, Craig's voice crackled over the air. "I'm here, Lucas. What's going on?"

"I found a campfire and some evidence that people were in the vicinity."

"Poachers?"

"Probably. Are you guys set up?"

"Yeah. We just finished." He gave Lucas the precise location of the camp.

Lucas looked at his watch. "All right. It's going to be dark soon. We'll come now." Altering direction slightly, they moved through the brush. Following behind Lucas, Kara was quiet as they walked, deep in her own thoughts.

Lucas looked back at her after a while. "You're so quiet I thought I'd lost you."

There was a flash of dimple in her cheek as her eyes met his. "No such luck, I'm afraid."

Lucas looked at her a moment longer and shook his head as he continued walking.

Kara watched him—the way he walked with such strong, purposeful strides; the way his sweat-soaked shirt fitted over his broad shoulders. She didn't know if it was his size or his attitude, but she knew she trusted him.

They walked into camp about half an hour later. Craig had chosen a spot in a low-grass area. Kara saw that several small tents had already been set up in a horseshoe pattern. A long portable table at one end of the site had several men sitting at it, talking and laughing as they cleaned their weapons.

While Kara stopped walking to look around, Lucas spotted Craig and headed for him. Quinn came out of one of the tents. "Kara! You took long enough to get here. How'd your first trek across the Serengeti go?"

"About the way you'd expect a first trek across the Serengeti to go."

"Meaning?"

"Meaning, my kingdom for a pair of real walking shoes."

"That bad, eh?"

"Oh, Quinn, if I don't get my hands on something to soak my feet in, I may never walk again."

"I'm sure they have something you can use. How was it being with Lucas all day?"

"Interesting," Kara said. "He's different than I thought he was."

"Is that good or bad?"

"Good." She switched her backpack to her other arm. "Is there someplace where I can get cleaned up? I can't remember ever being this filthy."

"Craig set up a place for us between our tents. Follow me."

Quinn led her across the camp to a tent at one end of the horseshoe. Next to the tent was a folding table that held a basin, washcloth and towel. Several jugs of water had been placed on the ground beside it. A sheet had been strung between her tent and Quinn's to shield them from the rest of the camp.

"What about the others?" Kara asked.

"The men all have the tables and basins. The sheet's here out of consideration for our womanhood."

"What about our things?"

"The shoulder bag with your clothes is already in your tent. I put it there myself."

"Thanks."

Darkness and the chill of night was settling over the camp. The sweet smell of an open fire was in the air. Someone called out that dinner was ready.

"Too late for a bath," Quinn said.

"I'll just wash my face and hands and be right out."

"Okay. I'll tell the others."

Kara poked her head through the flaps of her tent and looked around. It gave new meaning to the word tiny. There was room enough only for sleeping—and getting dressed if she could manage the required gymnastics. Bending over her bag, she took out her soap and stepped back outside behind the sheet to wash up and just put her feet in a basin of water for a few minutes.

When she joined the others, they were already lined up to get their food. Lucas was at the end of the line. He handed her a plate and utensils and waved her ahead of him.

"Thank you."

The cook, a very tall, very thin friendly fellow, ladled some kind of stew onto her plate and handed her a large chunk of bread. Kara dutifully followed the group to the table where they'd been cleaning their weapons earlier and sat on the end of the bench so she could watch the others. To her surprise, Quinn passed her to sit next to Lucas. Kara looked at their faces in the warm glow of a battery-powered lantern.

"From what I can tell," Lucas was saying, "the poachers are a day ahead of us. I think they're tracking a rhino. Maybe two. It's hard to tell because the tracks have been distorted."

"What are we going to do about it?" Craig asked.

"I want to pick up with Sudi and Ajani tomorrow where I left off today."

The two Africans nodded in acknowledgment.

"Craig, you, Kito and Lado follow about a mile behind with the flatbed truck. Keep in constant radio contact with those of us on foot. If there is a rhino out there and we find it first, we'll dart it and haul it back to Saragi before transporting it to a safety zone. Any questions?" He looked around at everyone.

Kara cleared her throat. "May I come with you?"

Lucas looked at her in surprise. "After today, you want to go back out there tomorrow?"

"Yes."

"I don't know. If there really are poachers out there it could be dangerous."

"As long as I don't get in your way, I think whether I go with you or not should be my decision."

"The operative phrase being, as long as you don't get in the way."

"And I won't. I held up fairly well today."

"Fairly," he agreed.

"If it counts for anything," Craig said, "I think you should let her go."

Lucas's utensils clattered onto his plate. "All right. If that's what you want. Now, let's all have an early night. Wake up is at dawn tomorrow." He left the table and the others followed suit, leaving Craig, Quinn and Kara alone at the table.

Craig looked at Quinn and smiled. "You don't want to strike out on foot, do you?"

"You've got to be kidding. I mean, I want to see Africa, but not too closely."

"Good. You can stay with me. May I walk you ladies to your tents?"

The three of them rose and walked leisurely across the darkened camp. Craig bade Kara and Quinn good-night and went to his tent. Kara lifted a lantern from a hook in front of her tent. It was the only light on in the entire camp.

Lucas was sitting in the dark outside his tent, directly across from Kara's. He had a lot on his mind. Almost absently, his gaze followed her to her tent and then to the basin behind the sheet. Kara set the lantern on the ground beside her, unaware that it projected her silhouette against the sheet.

Lucas watched her pour water into the basin, then lean her head over it to wash her hair. When she was finished, she wrapped her hair in a towel and removed her clothes. Wetting a washcloth and soaping it, she started with her face and made her way down her throat and breasts. The water felt good on her dusty skin despite the chill of the evening, and Kara took her time.

When she'd finished soaping herself, she filled the cloth with fresh water and squeezed it over herself, letting it run down her body.

The muscles in Lucas's jaw clenched as he watched. He rose from his chair and walked to the sheet. "Kara?" he said quietly so as not to wake the others.

She grabbed a towel and held it against herself. "Who's that?"

"Lucas."

She moved closer to the sheet and pulled a corner of it aside so she could see him. "What do you want?"

"I think you missed a spot behind your left ear."

She frowned at him. "What are you talking about?"

"Next time, either use a thicker sheet, or set the lantern so that your shadow isn't thrown against the material."

Kara gasped and instantly turned off the lantern. "How dare you spy on me!"

"I wasn't spying. I was sitting in front of my tent minding my own business when you thrust yourself into my consciousness."

Kara, still behind the sheet, closed her eyes. "You could have said something instead of just watching me."

"I'm saying something now."

"This is very embarrassing."

"Believe me, you have nothing to be embarrassed about. You're very lovely, Kara."

"That's hardly the point."

"Good night, Kara."

She heard his footsteps grow fainter as he headed out of camp. With the lantern still off, Kara briskly toweled herself off and put on a clean shirt, then went to her tent, dropped the mosquito netting around the cot and lay down.

She didn't like being caught off guard like that.

Not by Lucas.

Especially not by Lucas.

She wanted to think; needed to think. But her body let her down. The harder she tried to stay awake, the heavier her eyelids grew. It had been a very long, very exhausting day.

Lucas had gone for a walk to clear his head. There were things he wanted to accomplish in his life, and they left no room for any long-term involvement with a woman. An occasional affair, however, wasn't a problem.

But Kara wasn't the kind of woman a man had an affair with and then forgot. She was the kind of woman who could work her way into a man's soul—if he let her.

Lucas walked for more than an hour, then returned to camp. It was completely engulfed in darkness. He paused for a moment and looked at Kara's tent, then continued on to his own.

He'd already cleaned up earlier. Without taking off his clothes, he lay on his cot, one arm behind his head, and stared blindly into the darkness.

A loud howl sliced the night air. Kara sat straight up in bed, her heart pounding, very suddenly wide-awake.

There was another howl. It sounded like it was right outside her tent.

Kara carefully slid off her cot and groped her way through the darkness to her shoulder bag, looking for a weapon of some kind. Unfortunately, the most lethal thing she could find was a hairbrush.

Feeling a little silly, she gripped it by the handle and raised it ready to strike if it became necessary.

She waited, holding her breath, but there were no more howls.

On her knees, Kara made her way to her tent flap and opened it enough to peer outside. Her gaze moved slowly over the site, looking for something—anything—dangerous. Nothing seemed to be looking back at her.

She stayed there on her knees, hairbrush poised, for at least ten minutes, waiting for something to move. Nothing did. She lowered the brush, but stayed on her knees, alert and frightened. She was never going to be able to get to sleep.

Through the darkness, she focused on Lucas's tent. She'd feel safe with him. Taking a deep breath, she poised for flight and took off at a dead run, crashing unceremoniously through his unsecured tent flap.

"What the hell?" Lucas shouted as he sat up.

"It's just me," Kara said in a breathless whisper as she turned and looked cautiously outside to see if anything had followed her.

Lucas shook his head to clear the sleep away. "What are you doing?"

"There's an animal out there."

"I certainly hope so."

"I'm serious. It howled—and it sounded hungry."

"Oh, for..." Lucas sighed and dragged his fingers through his hair. "Is this the first time you've ever camped out?"

"Yes."

"Put the tent flap down."

"But..."

"Put it down, Kara."

She reluctantly let it fall back into place and turned toward Lucas. "I'm sorry if I woke you up."

"Don't worry about it."

She looked around the small dark tent. "I'll just sit in a corner or something until daylight. You won't even know I'm here."

"Oh, I'll know."

She crashed into something as she tried to make her way to a corner. "Ouch!"

Lucas rolled his eyes. "Come here."

"I'm fine."

"But I'm not. I'm never going to get back to sleep with you knocking around in the dark, so just come here and stop arguing about it."

Kara bit her lower lip in embarrassment. "I suddenly feel very silly. I shouldn't have come. I'll just go back to my own tent."

"And do what? Stare at the tent top for the rest of the night? You're already here and I'm already awake. Just come over to the cot and lie down so we can both get some sleep."

She reluctantly made her way toward his voice. "The cot's kind of small."

"Well, you can always sleep on the ground along with whatever else is there."

"No!" she said quickly as she found the cot with her groping hands and sat on the edge. "This will be fine."

She could feel his smile even in the darkness. "I thought it might be." Lucas laid down and moved his long body to the edge of the cot, then reached up and pulled Kara down beside him, her back to his chest. He pulled the thin blanket over both of them. "Comfortable?" he asked.

Kara swallowed hard. She could feel his strong body against the entire length of her own. If she thought the howling outside had set her heart pounding, that was nothing to what this man did to her. Her head rested on one of his arms, while his other arm lay in the curve of her waist. "Oh, yes." Her voice cracked and she cleared her throat. "I'm just fine."

Lucas's chin rested on her soft mass of hair. The clean smell of it filled his lungs. And it was impossible not to notice how perfectly her body fit against his. He could feel himself reacting.

So could Kara. Her own response was so strong that she trembled.

Lucas pulled the blanket up to her shoulders, though he understood very well that it wasn't the cold that made her tremble. "Good night, Kara," he said softly against her hair.

"Good night," she whispered back.

Amazingly, despite whatever other feelings she had, there was such a sense of safety with Lucas that her exhaustion finally took over and Kara fell asleep.

Lucas listened to the light sound of her breathing. Any tiredness he'd felt earlier was gone. He was surprisingly content just to lie quietly with her; to inhale the wonderful scent of her.

There was no sleep for Lucas that night.

Chapter Six

"Let's go!" Lucas said loudly as he shook Kara's shoulder. "This is your second call. You don't get a third."

Kara shot up in her cot with a gasp.

"Move it, woman!"

It took her a moment to get oriented. She realized quite suddenly that she was in her own tent. But how...? Lucas must have carried her. That was the only way. She'd been in such a sound sleep that she hadn't even been aware of it.

How embarrassing. The entire night was embarrassing. Whatever the reason for her going to his tent, it must look to Lucas as though she was throwing herself at him. And maybe she was.

Well, she just wouldn't say anything about it, and hope that he'd be enough of a gentleman to forget it, as well.

Stumbling to her feet, she quickly stripped off the shirt she used for pajamas and slipped into a clean pair of shorts and loose-fitting T-shirt. Bending over, she brushed her hair into a thick ponytail and fastened it with the grass Lucas had braided for her the day before.

"Are you coming, Ms. Stanhope?" Lucas bellowed from across the camp.

Kara grabbed her backpack and flew out of her tent, across the camp to where Lucas, Sudi and Ajani stood waiting, their rifles slung over their shoulders.

"I'm sorry," she said breathlessly.

"Don't be sorry," Lucas said, eyeing her backpack. "Do you still have your water from yesterday?"

"Yes."

"Then let's go. And make sure you keep up."

"But Quinn..."

"She'll be staying here with Craig and the others until we need them."

There was no time to say goodbye to anyone. Lucas and the others were already walking. Kara scrambled to catch up, and then had to scramble every few steps to stay caught up.

It was still early, but the sun was nearly all the way up. Kara could feel that the air was already heavy with heat and humidity and she knew by now that it was only going to get worse as the day wore on.

They made their way to where Lucas had broken off the search the day before, and picked it up from there. The three men fanned out, searching the ground for any tracks.

They had walked for more than two hours when Sudi stopped suddenly and kneeled to examine something. Kara, who'd been following closely behind him, stopped also and leaned over to look at the ground. "What is it?" she asked.

"Rhinos," he said. "Two of them." He called to Lucas and Ajani.

"It looks like an adult and a baby," Lucas said after a moment's glance. He straightened and followed the tracks for about fifty yards. "Damn." He stopped walking and picked something up from the ground.

"What is it?" Kara asked as she walked toward him.

"A cigarette butt."

"Poachers?"

"Poachers," he said grimly.

"Craig," he said into his walkie-talkie. "We have something."

"What is it?" Craig's voice came back almost immediately.

"Two rhinos have been this way and at least one poacher is right behind them."

"How long ago?"

"A day. Maybe less. I want you to circle around with the trucks, get ahead of us by about five miles, then come back in straight toward us. If the poachers are still out there, I want to try to trap them between us."

"All right. What about Kara?"

Lucas looked at her.

"I want to go with you," she said firmly.

"You'd be safer in the truck with Craig."

"What you're really saying is that I won't be in your way if I'm in the truck."

"That, too."

Kara's eyes looked directly into his. "I won't get in your way. I would never do anything to hinder your catching either the rhinos or the poachers. If I thought that was a factor, I'd leave right now, but I can take care of myself. You, Ajani and Sudi do what you need to and I'll follow quietly behind. You won't even know I'm here. Really."

Lucas studied her determined face. "Craig?" he said pushing the switch on the walkie-talkie, "Kara's staying with us."

"Are you sure you want to do that?"

"No, but that's the way it is."

"All right. We're out of here."

Kara, true to her word, stayed behind the others, not interfering. Every once in a while, Lucas would look back at her, just to make sure she was handling their pace.

They found the ashes from another fire—a very recent one, and followed the human trail up a slight hill and down again. Before Kara was all the way up the hill, she heard Lucas swear loudly.

Running, she made it over the crest and gasped at what lay below, about twenty feet away: A baby rhino, its body riddled with bullets from what had to be a machine gun, lay on its side. Its horns had been mercilessly hacked off with an ax. Kara had never seen anything so horrible, so heartbreaking. Tears streamed unchecked down her face, leaving trails in the dust on her cheeks, as she moved slowly forward.

Lucas placed himself between Kara and the little rhino. "There's no need for you to look at this."

She swallowed hard, her eyes meeting his. "What kind of man can do something like this?"

"The kind who doesn't give a damn about anything but money," he said with quiet fury. "The horns on that baby couldn't have weighed any more than four or five pounds."

Sudi walked toward them. "It's been dead for about four hours. There's no sign of the mother."

"She wouldn't have gone far from her baby. The poachers would know that, too. Let's try to find her." Lucas didn't sound very hopeful about finding her alive. He lifted Kara's face to his. With a gentleness that took her by surprise, he wiped away her tears with his thumbs. "Are you all right?"

"I will be."

"I know this is hard for you. It's still hard for me after ten years of seeing it."

She nodded.

His gaze moved slowly over her face and came to rest on her quivering lips. He rubbed his thumb over them. "This is no place for you," he said softly.

"You may be right. I wasn't expecting to see anything like that."

"Do you want to go back to Saragi? I can have one of the men take you."

A corner of her mouth lifted. "You're being nice to me again. I wish you wouldn't. It throws me off my stride."

"Which doesn't answer my question."

"I'm right where I want to be."

"You're very stubborn."

"I'm not usually."

"Come on, then. We've got to find the mother."

As soon as Lucas had turned away from her, Kara saw the baby rhino again. She wanted to look away, but couldn't. Instead of following Lucas, she went to the little rhino and knelt beside it. "I'm so sorry," she whispered as she rested her hand on its neck.

The air was still, as though in acknowledgment of death.

Lucas turned to say something to Kara, but she wasn't there. Starting to get annoyed, he backtracked a few yards and was about to shout her name, but stopped when he saw her.

Kara was oblivious to her surroundings as Lucas walked up behind her and rested his hand on her shoulder.

She turned her head and looked up at him. "How do you get past the anger, Lucas?"

"I don't."

She nodded as she rose. "Are you going to bury the baby?"

"Out here we tend to let nature take her course."

"I see."

"We can't lose any more time, Kara. Either come with me now or I'll have to make arrangements to send you back to Saragi."

"I'm coming."

Kara easily fell into step beside Lucas, her thoughts on the rhino. "Do you suppose the poachers have already found the mother?"

"It's a good bet."

"How could any man kill and butcher an animal that way and still sleep at night? And why? What's so important about a rhino's horn that it makes this kind of destruction so commonplace?"

"People pay thousands of dollars for rhino horns. They're believed by some to have medicinal powers. Other's think that when the horn is ground into a powder, it becomes an aphrodisiac. It's not true, of course, but it's difficult to change hundreds of years of beliefs in just one generation. In Kenya, just twenty years ago, more than ten thousand black rhinos roamed freely. Now there are fewer than five hundred left, most of them in sanctuaries with electrified fences to keep poachers out."

Kara looked at him in disbelief. "Fewer than five hundred?"

"It's incredible, isn't it?"

Sudi yelled something unintelligible at that moment and Lucas took off running. Kara followed closely behind. They found the African hunkered down in the tall grass behind a tree. At a signal from him, Lucas stopped running. He motioned for Kara to be still and quiet. Very slowly, bent at the waist so that he was somewhat hidden in the grass, he made his way to Sudi. Kara, again, was close behind, mimicking Lucas's movements.

"Can you believe it?" Sudi whispered, pointing.

In the clearing, alert, her head up so she could sniff the air, her large ears twitching, was the mother rhino.

Lucas unshouldered his dart-loaded rifle and took aim. An explosion rent the air. The rhino wheeled around twice and took off running. The four of them ran after her, crashing through the tall grass. Kara had trouble keeping up. Her lungs were burning from the effort, but she hung in.

They ran for more than a mile before finding the rhino again. She was just standing there, dazed. As they watched, her legs buckled under her and she rolled onto her side.

"Stay back," Lucas ordered Kara as the rest of them moved forward.

The rhino thrashed around, threatening anything that came near with her long needle-sharp horn.

Lucas got on his radio. "Craig, are you there?"

The radio crackled. "I'm here, Lucas."

"We've got one adult rhino here that needs to be transported."

"Give me your location."

Lucas did. It amazed Kara that he could not only give a location, but that Craig could find him out here in the middle of seemingly nowhere.

"We'll be there with the flatbed in fifteen minutes."

Lucas handed the radio to Sudi and moved closer to the rhino. The huge animal lay completely still except for breathing. He visually checked her over. "Look at that," he said, pointing to her hind quarters. "She was shot, but the bullet just grazed her."

Kara moved closer, too, so she could see what he was talking about. Sure enough, there was a wound.

He walked around behind the rhino to get a closer look. The rhino didn't move.

As he came around to her front, Lucas hunkered down near her head, keeping himself just out of reach of the horn. There was no movement.

Kara knelt next to him. "How long will she be immobilized?"

"Long enough to get her back to a pen in Saragi."

"And then what?"

"We'll make arrangements to have her transported to a sanctuary where she'll be safer. A little safer, anyway."

"May I touch her?" Kara asked.

Lucas moved his hand over the animal's shoulder. "Sure," he said.

Kara touched the rough, gray skin. "She's huge. I didn't realize."

"Haven't you ever seen one in a zoo?"

"Of course, but they look different in zoos—smaller."

"I hadn't thought about that, but I guess they would. There's nothing quite like being right next to an animal to give you a feel for the reality."

Sudi swung himself up into a tree and looked into the distance. "Here they come," he yelled after a few minutes.

Not long after that they heard the engines. Lucas rose and walked toward the noise to meet the men and bring them back to the rhino.

Craig winked at Kara as he pulled the Range Rover off to the side. Quinn got out and stood next to her to watch as the flatbed pulled up near the rhino.

Talking excitedly and moving fast, several of the men bound the rhino's feet and head with ropes. With surprising ease, they managed to maneuver a heavy sheet of canvas under the rhino, which they then attached to a pulley. The rhino, on its canvas bed, was hoisted into the air and swung onto the flatbed. Ropes were run from the slats in the sides of the truck to the ropes already securing the rhino to assure that it wouldn't hurt anyone or itself if it did wake from its drugged sleep. Another canvas was placed over the flatbed to protect the rhino from the harsh afternoon sun.

"Now what?" Kara asked Lucas.

"I go with the men in the flatbed to take the rhino back to Saragi. I have to make sure she doesn't have any emergencies because of the tranquilizer."

"And the rest of us?"

"Go back to camp. I'll return sometime tomorrow and we'll spend the day looking for the poachers."

Kara smiled. "Good. I was afraid they were going to get away with what they did."

"They just might," Lucas said.

"Unless, of course, they're still looking for the mother rhino," Craig said. "If so, we'll nail them."

"My guess is that they're long gone," Lucas said. "Look at how easily we found the rhino. And they were hours ahead of us. I think they stopped searching before we even got here."

"Or maybe they're just not good trackers," Craig suggested.

"That's a possibility, but not very likely."

"How long will you look for them?" Kara asked.

"We can only give it another day, then we have to get back to business."

"What?" Kara couldn't believe what she was hearing. "You're only going to spend one more day looking for the brutes who murdered that poor baby?"

Lucas sighed. It was tough to explain the real world to people who didn't live the life. "The most important thing right now is that this rhino is safe. The poachers could be anywhere and we don't have the manpower to spend endless hours scouring the Serengeti in order to find them."

"So you're going to let them get away with it?" she asked indignantly.

"I'm going to do the best I can to see that they don't. All I'm doing right now is explaining the realities of the situation to you. This isn't some television show where we can wrap it up in a nice neat ending in one hour."

She didn't say anything.

"Kara," he explained with surprising patience, "there's a limit to what we can do. We don't have the money and we don't have the manpower."

"So if we don't find them tomorrow, they'll be free to kill again."

"In all likelihood. And when we finally catch them, there'll be others to take their place."

Her eyes stung with tears. "It just isn't right, Lucas."

"No, it isn't," he said softly. "And we're trying to change things, but it's difficult. We're constantly playing catch-up, and we're falling further and further behind. You've now seen firsthand the kind of ruthlessness we're up against."

"No wonder you are the way you are."

He lifted an eyebrow. "The way I am?"

"I don't think I need to go into detail here. Besides, you know exactly what I mean."

"Don't you like the way I am?" he asked innocently.

"I didn't yesterday."

Sudi walked quickly toward them. "We should be leaving."

"Do you want to go back to camp, or to Saragi with me?" Lucas asked her.

"Back to camp," Kara said without hesitation. "I want to be with you when you catch those guys tomorrow."

"If," he corrected.

Kara smiled at him. "When."

"I think I'll go back to Saragi," Quinn said. "I've had enough of the great outdoors for one lifetime."

"Oh," Kara said, suddenly contrite, "I'm sorry. I wasn't thinking. I'll go back with you."

"You don't have to."

"Of course, I do. We're supposed to be experiencing this together."

"You really don't have to. Just because I want to go back to where it's—and I can't believe I'm saying this—reasonably civilized."

Kara smiled at her. "What a difference a day makes."

"You can say that again. Besides, I want to get away from Craig."

"Get away from him? He's delightful."

"Then let him delight you for a while. I've had quite enough for one vacation."

"I was kind of hoping the two of you..."

Quinn raised her hand. "Don't even say it. Besides, if I were going to allow myself to become interested in someone here, it would be Lucas, not Craig."

Kara's eyes went to Lucas, in the back of the flatbed checking on the rhino. "Lucas?"

"At least he's interesting."

"But you're not seriously..."

"Don't be ridiculous."

Kara nodded.

Quinn tapped Kara on the shoulder. "And don't you be ridiculous, either."

"Me?"

"I'm not blind. I've seen the way you look at the man. He's not your type. He'll never be your type."

"Perhaps that's what I find so attractive about him."

"Don't let yourself get involved with him."

Kara eyed her sister. "Well, aren't you assertive all of a sudden."

"I just don't want you to get hurt. Besides, I can't have you spending the rest of your life in this place. I need you too much. You're my rock. I don't know what I would have done without you this past year. I don't think I would have made it." Quinn hugged her. "I still need you."

Kara silently hugged her back.

Quinn turned away from her and climbed into the cab of the flatbed.

Lucas said something to Sudi, jumped down from the back of the flatbed and walked over to Craig. They spoke with quiet intensity for a few minutes, then Lucas came to Kara. "You stay out of trouble," he said.

"I will."

"Don't do anything stupid."

She smiled at him, but her heart wasn't in it. There were times when she felt like a prisoner of her own life. "The problem is recognizing that it's stupid before I do it."

He shook his head. "Why do I have this sinking feeling that leaving you out here like this is a mistake?"

"I don't know."

Lucas reached out and touched her dirt-streaked cheek. "You need another bath. But this time make sure you don't have an audience."

Her cheeks grew pink.

"Don't be embarrassed. I wasn't."

Her cheeks grew pinker. "You're a horrible man."

"And despite that, you find yourself intrigued, don't you, Kara? Or is it because of that?"

Kara looked into his blue eyes and knew that it was true. Then she saw Quinn watching them from the truck. "Goodbye," she said abruptly. "And please be nice to my sister on the drive to Saragi. If you give her a chance, I think you'll find she's a wonderful person."

Lucas's hand fell to his side. "I wish I could shake this feeling that I should take you with me back to Saragi."

"I'll be fine. Really. I can take care of myself."

"I've seen how you take care of yourself."

"And if something does happen, that'll be one less tourist you'll have to worry about."

Lucas didn't smile.

"That was supposed to be funny."

"Just watch yourself."

She frowned. "I will."

Lucas walked back to Craig.

"What is it?" Craig asked.

"I have a bad feeling. I can't explain it. Just keep your eye on Kara. Don't let her out of your sight."

Craig looked at his friend curiously. In all the years they'd known each other, this was the first time Lucas had shown this kind of concern about a tourist.

"I know," Lucas said, reading his thoughts. "I can't explain it. I don't even want to try. Just watch her for me."

"All right. Consider it done."

Lucas climbed behind the steering wheel. Sudi banged twice on the roof and the flatbed lurched forward.

Kara watched until it disappeared into a cloud of dust.

Craig came up beside her and put his arm around her shoulders. "I've seen happier expressions on the faces of death row inmates." He gave her a squeeze.

Kara attempted a smile.

He shook his head. "Pitiful. What's wrong?"

"This is turning out to be quite a holiday."

"In what sense?"

"Self-revelations."

"Anything I'd be interested in?"

Kara lifted her shoulders. "I don't know, Craig. You go through life and think you know yourself pretty well, and then something happens and you realize suddenly that the person you thought you were is someone completely different." She turned her head to look at him. "Does that make any sense at all?"

"It sounds a little schizophrenic to me."

"Yes, it does, doesn't it?"

"Does this, by any chance, have something to do with my partner?"

"It has everything to do with him."

"You haven't fallen for him, have you?" Craig asked.

"I hope not."

"Don't you know?"

"Oh, I know what I feel. What I need is some time alone to think about what I'm feeling, to analyze it and try to understand it."

So that's what was going on, Craig thought with an inward smile. *Talk about opposites attracting.* "Can I assume we're talking about Lucas?"

"I don't want to feel anything for him," Kara said softly, watching as the last of the dust settled back to earth. "But I don't know that that's anything a person has control over."

"Perhaps."

"But whether it's controlled or not, a person can't just set aside other responsibilities."

"Now we're talking about your sister."

She looked at Craig. "I only came here for a holiday as a favor to Quinn. I never intended this as a life-altering experience."

"You think too much. Just go with the flow."

"That's irresponsible."

"Sometimes you have to be irresponsible. And sometimes you have to stop putting your own life on hold in order to take care of someone else."

Kara didn't say anything.

Chapter Seven

Kara lay on her cot, unable to sleep. She tossed from one side to the other, listening to the distant rumble of thunder.

She couldn't get Lucas out of her thoughts. She kept remembering how it felt to fall asleep in his arms. There was something so right about being with him. And when he touched her, no matter how casually, and no matter how her heart raced, it felt good and natural. They were connected. Despite the differences between them, there was something there, intangible but ever present. It was frightening to feel that way about a man she barely knew.

And yet in some ways she knew him so very well.

With a sigh, she picked up a flashlight and shone it on her watch. Two o'clock in the morning. This was ridiculous. She was never going to get to sleep like this.

Sitting up, she reached for her shorts and slipped them on, then pulled on her socks and shoes.

Stepping out of her tent, she looked around. Everything was in darkness. She was the only one still up.

What she needed, Kara thought, was a book. A nice, thick, boring book. But she hadn't brought one with her. Short of that, maybe a walk would help. Anything to tire her so much that she'd stop thinking.

With her flashlight in hand, she headed out of camp, not intending to walk far. Her steps crunched through the dried grass, but the night noises of the plain masked the sound. With the beam of her flashlight bouncing off the scattered trees, Kara picked her way along what seemed at the time almost a path. She kept reminding herself to pay attention to where she was going, but no sooner did she have the thought than the problem that was keeping her awake overpowered her good intentions.

It wasn't a very well-known fact because Kara had always tried to hide it under a mask of efficiency, but she was a dreamy sort of person. She was better at taking care of other people than she was at taking care of herself.

The thunder cracked and rumbled over the plain. The earth literally shook from the force of the airborne explosion.

Kara didn't usually like storms, but tonight she welcomed the violence. She felt at one with it.

The beam of her flashlight picked out a flat-topped boulder and Kara headed for it. It was easy to clamber up its four-foot side to sit on top of it. The night air was warmer than usual, and alive, as though charged by the distant storm.

She lay back on the rock and stared at the sky. Lightning fingered its way across the blackness, lighting the plain in erratic flashes. The thunder cracked and rumbled, vibrating right through her, but there was no rain. Kara found herself vaguely wondering if the lightning was caused by heat or whether the rains were on the way. She hoped it was the rains so she could see the Serengeti in bloom before she left.

Kara listened to the night noises. She was getting used to them. They didn't frighten her anymore. In fact, they were actually like a sedative, seeping into her, slowing down her pulse, relaxing her.

But there was no escaping her thoughts.

And they were all about Lucas Pierson.

She couldn't get away from him. Every time she closed her eyes, he was there. Every time she opened them, he was there.

It was as though something inside her recognized that the man she'd spent twenty-five years waiting for had suddenly walked into her life. How could something like that be explained?

Kara sniffed. There was an odd smell, as though something was burning.

She sat up and sniffed again. Yes, something was definitely burning.

With a frown creasing her forehead, Kara looked out over the plain. She didn't see anything unusual. And yet...

She turned her head to look in the other direction. Lightning must have sparked a grass fire because the plain was burning. The fire line couldn't have been more than half a mile away, and it was moving in her direction.

There was no way she could get to camp. The fire was between her and it. But at least she didn't have to worry about the others. They'd be all right as long as the winds didn't shift and force the flames in the other direction.

Her mind raced. She couldn't get around the fire. It stretched in a straight line for nearly as far as the eye could see, though it was impossible to see how deep it was.

Her only option was to stay ahead of it.

Kara slid off the rock and started running.

"Don't panic," she told herself breathlessly as she ran. "Don't panic. Just keep moving."

Now, for the first time, she began to understand the phrase "raced like wildfire." The grass was so dry and brittle that the mere suggestion of heat caused it to burst into flames. It moved so fast that it seemed to be chasing Kara. No matter how fast she ran, the fire kept getting closer.

With her lungs ready to burst, Kara stopped and looked around, searching for a safe place. Somewhere to hide until the fire was gone. She wrapped her arms around her aching stomach. Her breathing was ragged and painful. "Oh, God, oh, God, oh, God!" she yelled, panic rising to the surface. She didn't know what to do.

She closed her eyes and forced herself to calm down. If she let herself get hysterical it would be all over for her.

The sun had come up and she hadn't even noticed. Lightning rent the sky and thunder cracked.

"Can anyone hear me?" she screamed.

She listened for an answer, but she could only hear the fire.

"Lucas!" she screamed louder.

The hot wind from the wall of fire hit her full in the face. Kara gasped at the unexpectedness of it. She couldn't just stand there and wait to be swallowed by the flames.

Adrenaline poured into her. She started running again, crashing through the grass, looking for sanctuary but not really expecting to find any. Dozens of small animals scurried for shelter.

Suddenly a hand caught her from behind.

Kara whirled around, ready to fight, not knowing what to expect. It was Lucas! "What are you doing here?" she gasped.

"Looking for you." He grabbed her hand and started pulling her along behind him. "I knew it. I knew it even before I left yesterday. If there's trouble to be found, you're right in the middle of it."

"I just went for a walk," she said breathlessly as she tried to keep up with him. It was more self-defense than anything else. He was so mad at her she had the feeling that if she fell, he'd just drag her along behind him.

"What are you doing back here so early?"

"I told you, I just had a feeling something was wrong. As soon as the rhino could stand on her own, I headed back for camp instead of spending the night at Saragi."

"Are the others safe?"

"Yes. The fire's moving away from them."

"How did you get through it?"

"I found a hole in the fire wall."

"Can't we go back that way?"

"It closed up almost as soon as I was through it. There's no going back. Now be quiet. Save your breath for running."

And run they did, for what seemed like miles. They reached the dry riverbed she and Lucas had crossed two days before. Stopping in the middle of it, Kara dropped his hand and doubled over, gasping for air. Lucas was breathing hard, too, but he stood straight, looking around.

"Why are we stopping here?" Kara panted.

"There's no grass here. No trees."

"And no water."

"You're missing the point," he said. "There's nothing here that will burn. But it's too narrow."

"Too narrow for what?"

Lucas didn't explain as he grabbed her hand again and started running down the riverbed's winding path until he found a spot that was nearly fifty feet from bank to bank. "This should do it," he said.

Kara looked at him in astonishment. "This should do it? We're stopping here? We're just going to stand here and wait for the fire?"

"We're going to sit here and wait for the fire." He put his hands on her shoulders and pressed her to the ground. "Pull your knees up."

She did.

Lucas sat behind her, opened his legs wide and pulled her between them so that her back was against his chest. "Wrap your arms around your legs and lower your head so that your forehead is resting on your knees."

"What..."

"Don't ask questions. Just do it."

She did it.

Lucas wrapped his own arms around Kara and put his head on top of hers. "The fire'll be here soon, but we're going to be all right," he said, his mouth close to her ear. "Don't be afraid."

Kara moved back so that she was pressed more closely against his chest. Lucas wrapped his arms around her even more tightly.

The fire had raced to meet them. Kara could hear the sap popping in the burning trees and limbs crashing to the ground. Lucas lifted his head slightly and so did Kara. At a narrow bend in the riverbed not far from where she was, flames shot high into the air. Burning leaves and grass were carried across the riverbed by the winds and ignited the other side.

Then the fire reached them.

The heat was unbearable. Kara buried her face in her arms. Breathing was difficult.

The roar of the flames was deafening. Kara was sure that they were going to be burned alive.

She waited for the pain.

But after what seemed like an eternity, the furious noise began to die down.

She felt Lucas raise his head. Kara raised hers also, her eyes narrowed against the stinging smoke.

The riverbank where the fire had been was now a charred, smoking mess. Some trees still burned, but the wall of flames had burned itself out.

She turned her head to look on the other side. Where they were, the flames hadn't been strong enough to make the leap, but two separate lines of fire that had made it across the narrower parts of the riverbed were straining to meet each other to once again create a solid wall.

Lucas rose first and pulled Kara up after him. "Are you all right?" he asked, cupping her soot-covered face in his hands and looking into her eyes.

She put her hands over his as she nodded. "And you?"

"Fine."

"I can't believe we're alive. I can't believe you came for me."

Without warning, Lucas pulled her into his arms and crushed her lips beneath his. There was no thought, just raw passion, and Kara's body responded all on its own. Her lips parted beneath his, welcoming him. Lucas moved his hands to her hips and pulled her body tightly against his until he could feel every curve, and he knew she could feel how much he wanted her right then and there. It was as though the fire had entered the two of them and still raged.

They both dropped to their knees. Lucas left her lips to kiss the long line of her throat as Kara arched her back and tilted her head.

He tangled his fingers in her long hair with one hand, pulling her mouth to his, and moved the other down her bare back, over her hip and slowly up the inside of her thigh.

Kara opened her eyes and looked into his.

Lucas saw something in those green depths that gave him pause.

"Don't stop," she whispered.

Lucas sighed as he wrapped her in his arms and just quietly held her.

"What's wrong?" Kara asked, searching his face for some clue. "What did I do?"

Lucas shook his head. "You didn't do anything. This just isn't right."

"I think I'm in love with you," she said softly.

"Don't say that, Kara."

"That's why I couldn't sleep last night. That's why I went for a walk this morning. I was trying to sort things out."

"There's nothing to sort out."

"Don't you feel anything for me?"

Lucas sat back on his heels and looked at her. "I feel about you the way any man would feel about a beautiful woman."

"But just now—"

"Just now," he interrupted her, "I wanted to make love to you. We both nearly died, and the most natural thing in the world after an experience like that is to want to make an intimate connection. It would have been a mistake, at least for you."

"But not for you?"

He touched her cheek. "For me, it would have been just a physical connection, nothing more."

Kara swallowed hard. It had never occurred to her that when she finally fell in love with a man, he wouldn't love her back. "I see."

"I hope so."

Thunder cracked overhead.

"We should try to get back to the others," Lucas said, turning away from her. "We can follow the riverbed for a while."

It was tough not to feel humiliated, but Kara tried as she followed along behind him. It wasn't as though there was someplace she could hide. The best she could do was pretend it had never happened.

But she knew that it had.

As they walked Kara noticed that the bright morning sun was being increasingly blocked out by storm clouds until it seemed like night. Lightning flashed behind the clouds, lighting the sky, and thunder rumbled through the earth.

The drops of rain, when they finally fell, were huge. They slapped against Kara with stinging force. And as they hit the still-hot trees and grass along the riverbank, there was a hissing noise followed by clouds of steam.

Lucas didn't say anything. He just kept walking and so did Kara.

Actually, once she got used to the force of it, Kara rather enjoyed it. The surprisingly cold water felt good against her sooty skin and hair. And she'd given up days earlier worrying about how she looked. Comfort had become much more important.

The downside to the wonderful rain was that the riverbed was turning to muck. Lucas climbed up the riverbank and held out his hand for Kara. She hesitated before letting him help her.

"I won't bite," he said.

"You have before." She put her hand in his and let him pull her up.

"The rain should have dampened the ground enough so that it's safe to walk on."

"You sound as though this happens all the time."

"We have a lot of fires. Usually, though, we're not caught in the middle of them."

"How come none of them have burned Saragi?"

"We have a firebreak and no trees close to the buildings. Watch your step," he said, taking her arm and helping her over a fallen acacia limb that was still smoldering in the rain.

The rain came down even harder. And frankly, it didn't feel so good anymore. Enough was enough.

Where there had been only cracked, dried mud in the riverbed earlier, there was now a rivulet of fast-running water. It grew quickly in the heavy downpour until there was a real river there. Kara couldn't believe how fast it had gone from nothing to something dangerous.

"Do you know where you're going?" she called to Lucas over the sound of the rain.

"Yes."

"Would you mind sharing it with me?"

"Back to the camp."

"Are you sure it's this way?"

"I'm sure."

They started walking away from the river.

As quickly as the rain had come, it left. The dark clouds disappeared. The lightning that had been flashing since the early hours of the morning faded away.

But Kara, as she pushed her dripping hair out of her face, was horrified by the destruction left behind by the fire. "How long will this take to recover?" she asked.

"You'll see new growth by tomorrow."

"Tomorrow?" she repeated, shocked.

"It'll take years, of course, for the trees to make a comeback, but the grass will start growing right away."

"How can that be?"

"These fires are quick. They burn the surface but don't affect any seeds lying just beneath the surface. In some areas of the plain, the native Africans start fires deliberately to burn off the tall, dried grass so that there's room for the new grass to grow."

"What about the animals?"

"They have an amazing amount of ingenuity. The first time I saw one of these fires, I thought the animals would die. But very few do. They seem to know quite naturally what they have to do to protect themselves."

"As opposed to some people," Kara said dryly.

Lucas smiled at her. "Exactly."

Their eyes met and held. Kara looked away first. "Did you bring Quinn back to camp with you or did she stay at Saragi?"

"She's at Saragi. I think she's had enough of African-style camping for this lifetime."

"Did she say that?"

"She said enough to let me know that this isn't her idea of paradise."

"Is it yours?" Kara asked.

"It might have been fifty years ago. Now everything seems to be a struggle."

"And yet you wouldn't live anywhere else."

"This is my home. It has been from the moment I first set foot on the land."

"It's more than your home," Kara said quietly. "It's your mistress."

He turned his head and looked into her eyes. "That's right, Kara."

Craig and Ajani came crashing over a hill. Craig saw Kara first, ran over to her, picked her up off the ground and swung her in a circle. "There you are! I thought we were going to find the two of you burned to a crisp."

Kara laughed as he set her back on the ground. "A little singed, perhaps."

"And where exactly did you wander off to after I'd tucked you safely in your tent?"

"I couldn't sleep so I went for a walk. Everything would have been fine if it hadn't been for the fire."

"Next time I'll tether you to a tent stake." Craig shook his head as he looked at Lucas. "And you. After years of living out here, you should know better than to go tearing off alone like that when there's a fire."

"You were too slow."

"We were taking proper precautions."

"She would have been dead."

Craig looked at Kara. She nodded. "If this is as far as you've come since the fire, I would have been toast by now."

He looked at her more closely. "Are you sure you're all right?"

"I'm sure."

He sighed. "Well, that's more than I can say for our poachers."

"What do you mean?" Lucas asked.

"We found their bodies about half a mile back. They were still in camp. I don't think they knew what hit them."

"How many?"

"Three."

"Recognizable?"

"I'm afraid not."

"Then we've got nothing to keep us out here," Lucas said. "Let's head back for Saragi."

The four of them slogged their way through the soggy burned grass for another hour and a half. The burned plain suddenly disappeared and, as though a line had been drawn, they entered a part untouched by fire. Camp was another thirty minutes away.

Craig shot his rifle into the air to alert the others that they were back and in a little while they straggled into camp, as well.

Avoiding eye contact with Lucas, Kara helped break the camp down and pack it up. She did fine as long as someone told her what to do. It wasn't as difficult as it looked.

But she didn't really have to worry about avoiding Lucas. He was doing fine on his own, staying away from her.

Craig looked from one to the other of them. "Is something going on that I should know about?" he asked Lucas.

Lucas grunted as he heaved a heavy table into the back of a truck. "What are you talking about?"

"You and Kara. Things seem a bit strained between the two of you."

"Everything's fine."

Craig handed him a bench. "You're a fool if you let her get away from you."

"It's none of your business."

"You're my friend, Lucas. I care about you. I don't want to see you make the mistake of a lifetime."

Lucas shoved the bench into the truck.

"She's perfect for you. Surely you can see that?"

Lucas, his jaw clenched, looked at his friend. "What I see is a harsh, unforgiving land and a future of hard work and heartbreak. Whatever I feel for Kara doesn't matter. This is no place for her. The life is too hard. You've seen what's happened to us over the past ten years. There are days when we get back to Saragi that we're so drained of emotion there's nothing left in us to share with someone else. What woman in her right mind would willingly put herself through what we've been through? And what kind of man would ask a woman he loved to make that kind of sacrifice for him?"

Chapter Eight

When they got back to Saragi, Kara nearly jumped out of the truck she'd been riding in with Craig. Quinn came running out of the house to meet her. "Oh, I'm so glad to see you! I heard there was a fire."

"I'm all right," Kara said. "I just want to get cleaned up."

Lucas parked his Rover behind Craig's and climbed out. Without looking at or speaking to anyone, he strode around to the back of the house.

"What's going on?" Quinn asked.

"Nothing." Kara attempted a smile but couldn't quite pull it off.

Nothing certainly seemed like something, but Quinn didn't press. She looked over her sister's shoulder to Craig. He pointed toward the game room and she nodded. "You really do need a shower, Kara. You look as though you've been painted with soot."

As soon as Kara had disappeared around the veranda, Quinn met Craig in the game room. "So?" she asked, perching on the arm of the couch and looking at him as he poured himself a soda. "What's going on?"

"Your sister and Lucas apparently had a falling out."

Quinn smiled. "They're always having a falling out."

"But this one was different."

"Different how?"

"Unless I miss my guess, they're in love with each other."

Quinn's expression was incredulous. "Oh, come on. I can understand an attraction, but love? The two of them have absolutely nothing in common."

"Since when do people need to have something in common in order to fall in love?"

"I did with my husband. We agreed on everything."

"Then you and your husband were unique and I congratulate you, but I don't think you should base the probable success of other relationships on your own."

"But I..."

"Kara isn't you. Her time out here has changed her. I don't know her very well, but even I can see that."

"Maybe so. But when we get back to civilization, she'll change back."

Craig finished his cola and set the empty glass on the bar. "Well, Quinn, I can see that the two of us are at conversational cross-purposes."

"Meaning?"

"I wanted to talk to you about getting the two of them together, but you obviously don't want that at all."

"What I want is what's best for my sister, and Lucas most definitely isn't it."

Craig looked at her in surprise. "Well, well. You're a very determined woman."

"I can be."

"And yet Kara somehow feels she needs to take care of you."

"We take care of each other. We're the only family we've got."

"And your version of taking care of Kara is to make her feel responsible for your emotional well-being?"

"I've been ill. My husband died, you know."

"But you're better now, aren't you? A lot better than you let on to Kara."

"I love my sister," Quinn said.

"Then maybe you should think about what's best for her for a change." He inclined his head toward her. "Good afternoon."

Quinn sat silently in the game room for a long time, then went onto the veranda and stared out at the plain. There was no way she would allow Kara to stay here. No way. Kara would never be happy living in this place.

* * *

Kara finished her shower and dressed in a man's oversize shirt that she tucked into the waistband of her jeans. She wasn't really in the mood for human companionship. Besides, she wanted to check on the puppy.

She saw Ajani ahead of her walking toward the animal compound as she stepped off the veranda. "Ajani!"

"Hello," he said with a large smile. "You're looking a little better." His English had a touch of a British accent.

"I'm feeling a little better. How's the rhino?"

"Not a happy camper, as the saying goes. Come. I'll show you."

They walked to about the middle of the compound where there was a heavily barricaded pen made of thick posts sunk into the ground and wired together. Something crashed into the side and the whole thing shook.

Ajani climbed onto a platform about halfway up the posts, then held out his hand to help Kara up.

"You see," he said as he pointed down at the rhino. "She's very unhappy."

"She probably wonders what happened to her baby."

The pen was small and didn't leave the rhino much room to maneuver, but the rhino herself was huge and when she threw herself against the posts, the earth shook.

"How come I've heard so little about the devastation of the rhino population, yet so much about elephants?"

Ajani smiled. "Elephants are more sympathetic creatures. More photogenic. It's easier to get people interested in helping pretty, nice animals."

Kara looked at the rhino closely. "I think she's lovely. Odd looking, certainly, but lovely."

"There's also the small matter of a nasty temper."

The rhino slammed into the pen again.

"You'd have a nasty temper, too, if you were locked up like this."

"True. But, quite frankly, this isn't an animal you want to mess with even when it's not locked up."

"When will you be transporting her?" Kara asked.

"Early tomorrow morning."

"Is Lucas going?"

"Yes," said Lucas from below her, "I'm going."

Startled, Kara looked down at him. Her heart beat faster. "May I go so I can see what . . . ?"

"No."

"But . . ."

"No."

Ajani looked at the two of them and tried not to smile.

"Why can't I go?" Kara asked.

Lucas looked up at Kara and straight into her eyes. "Because you're constantly getting into trouble and I just don't have the time for it anymore."

Kara really couldn't say much about that. Trouble *did* seem to come looking for her.

"Ajani, I need you to help me with one of the giraffes."

"Sure." Ajani hopped off the platform and the two men walked away.

The rhino hit the logs again and shook the pen. Kara caught herself on the end of one of the logs and kept watching the rhino. She still couldn't fathom that there were so few of them left in the wild. Something had to be done.

She heard some excited voices behind her and turned to find Sudi and another man chasing after two baby elephants who were tearing through the compound, their little trunks flying.

Kara jumped off the platform and ran after them.

Ajani and Lucas had apparently heard the commotion, too, and they came running out, heading the little fellows off and into a roomy pen. Kara got there just as the gate was being shut. "Where did you find them?" Kara asked.

"They found us," Sudi said, gasping for air. "I don't know whether they're lost or their mothers are dead."

"How will you find out?"

"If the mothers show up looking for them, we'll find out real fast."

"And if not?"

"We'll take care them."

Kara leaned over the low pen and held out her hand. Both babies came to her and ran their trunks over her bare arm to get to know the smell of her. "This place is like an orphanage," she said. "A place where babies can come to be fed and protected. I'd hate to think what would happen to them if you weren't here."

"That's why we'll always be here," Lucas said as he climbed into the pen with the elephants and started a careful examination.

"And if you run out of money?"

"We'll find a way. We always have."

Kara watched as he went over each animal. "Sudi," he finally said, "these two are still nursing. Mix some milk with meal and give it to them right away."

Sudi ran off.

"What can I do to help?" Kara asked.

"You could go back to Chicago," he suggested without a hint of a smile.

Kara couldn't hide the hurt in her eyes.

"Oh," Lucas said as he straightened away from the elephant, "don't look at me like that."

"How should I look at you?"

"Angrily."

"Isn't that interesting. I thought you were *trying* to hurt me. You're doing a fine job of it if that's not your object."

Lucas walked over to her. The elephants followed and started sniffing her with their trunks again. "I guess what I'm trying to do is get you angry enough to leave here."

"Why?"

"I think what happened between us this morning is sufficient explanation."

"What's wrong with what happened between us?"

"I'm not going to get involved with you."

"How involved can you get in three weeks?"

"More than I choose to."

"I think," Kara said as one of the little elephants wrapped his trunk around her arm and pulled her closer to the gate, "that you'd discover that I'm really a rather decent human being if you'd give yourself a chance. You might even find that you like me."

"I don't care whether you're decent and I don't want to like you."

"What are you afraid of, Lucas?"

Lucas came out of the pen, closed the gate and stood in front of Kara. His blue eyes were hooded. "Don't challenge me, Kara. You might not like the end result."

Kara's heart thumped against her ribs as she watched him walk away. No one had ever had the effect on her that this man had. It was confusing, and more than a little frightening.

One of the elephants reached a trunk into her hair and started sniffing. It tickled and Kara laughed.

But she was still thinking about Lucas.

She stayed with the elephants all afternoon, watching how they were fed and then playing with them. They were absolutely fearless and adorable, and incredibly full of affection.

When it was time for dinner, she cleaned herself up, changed into a light, flowing skirt and blouse, and went to the game room. Quinn was standing near the bookcase looking at titles, but turned when Kara walked in.

"Where have you been all afternoon?" she asked as Kara went to the bar and poured herself a glass of mineral water.

"In the animal compound. Two baby elephants came in today. You should go look at them."

"I'm sure they are magnificent."

Kara took her mineral water to the couch and sat down. "It's been a long day. I'm tired."

The cheetah, who'd been lounging in a chair, rose, stretched and jumped onto the couch beside Kara.

"It looks like you've found a friend," Quinn said dryly.

Kara looked down at the cheetah and smiled. "Sophia's beautiful, isn't she?"

"I think I'd like her better if she were a coat."

"Quinn! That's an awful thing to say!" Kara put her hand protectively on the cat's neck.

"I know, I know. Your consciousness has been raised." She looked at the cat and sighed. "I guess I just don't have a lot of empathy for animals who would be happy to have me as an hors d'oeuvre."

"Sophia's a pussycat—so to speak."

"You can hang out with her if you want, but I think I'll take a pass."

"You don't like it here at all, do you?" Kara asked.

"I'm counting the days until we leave." She carried a book to a chair and sat down. "You, on the other hand, seem to be thriving."

"I love it here. I feel like I'm home."

Quinn rolled her eyes.

"And you, my sister, are already looking and sounding stronger."

"Purely self-defense. If you're weak out here, you'll get swallowed alive."

They heard Hilda and Bertie before they saw them. When they walked in, Hilda was actually smiling.

Kara started to rise so they could have the couch, but Hilda waved her back down. "Please, stay where you are. Bertie and I can sit elsewhere."

"Are you enjoying your stay?" Kara asked.

"It's been absolutely fascinating," Hilda said as she sank into a chair. "I'm afraid you're missing the boat by not going on these day-long safaris with us. Joe's been a wonderful guide. And this is quite a place."

"Worth the hardship?" Kara asked.

"Well, I'd rather be venturing out from a nice, modern hotel and returning to one at night, but this will do for now."

Craig walked in and smiled at them. "Sorry I'm late. What can I get everyone?"

Kara raised her glass. "I'm all set, thank you."

Once Hilda had started talking, she didn't stop. They heard about every animal, every snippet of conversation, every geological formation that was even the least bit out of the ordinary.

Lucas walked in without saying anything to anyone and went to a desk at the far end of the room.

Kara tried not to stare at him, but her eyes kept wandering in his direction.

Quinn noticed, and her lips tightened.

Dinner that night was a classic American meal—hamburgers and french fries. Instead of eating at the table, they held their plates on their laps, except for Lucas, who ate at his desk.

Hilda continued talking.

As night fell and the lights inside the game room went on, Craig turned on some music. "Let's dance," he said to Quinn.

She looked up at him in surprise. "I beg your pardon?"

"Let's dance. Come on," he said as he took her hand and pulled her to her feet.

"But I don't..."

"You don't what? Dance?" He twirled her out and then pulled her back into his arms. "You most certainly do. And very beautifully."

Quinn laughed and shook her head. It was hard not to be charmed by him.

After a few minutes, Hilda and Bertie joined them. They were an odd-looking couple, but they somehow suited each other.

Kara looked at Lucas. He was still at his desk, his back to the room, writing, his food practically untouched. She set her plate on the coffee table and walked outside. Sophia followed her.

Together they walked to the rocks, but this time Kara didn't climb them. She just stood beside them and looked at the sliver of moon. The music from the house drifted to her. She closed her eyes and swayed gently from side to side.

A strong arm slipped around her waist.

Kara's eyes flew open to find Lucas looking down at her.

He didn't say anything as their bodies began swaying together. Neither did Kara, for fear she'd break the spell and he'd disappear into the night from which he'd come.

He wrapped one arm around her slender waist. Taking her free hand in his, he held her palm against his chest, his own hand over hers.

With only the moonlight and Sophia as their audience, their bodies touching, Lucas and Kara moved rhythmically together.

Kara rested her cheek on his shoulder. Lucas released her hand and moved his own hand to her hair, tangling his fingers in the curls.

The cheetah watched from the rocks above as the couple slowly circled.

And then the music stopped.

Lucas gazed down at Kara in the moonlight.

She wished she could see his eyes. What was he thinking about?

He cupped her face in his hands and felt her smooth skin beneath his gentle thumbs.

His hands fell to his sides, and as silently as he'd come, he left.

Kara stood staring after him, unaware that she wouldn't see him again for nearly two weeks.

Unaware that her sister stood on the veranda watching the shadowy figures in the moonlight and was anything but happy about it.

Kara wrapped her arms around herself and leaned against the boulders, staring out at the plain into which Lucas had disappeared. She'd had trouble understanding her reaction to Lucas. He made her feel things she'd never felt before.

But there was no more confusion.

She was in love with him.

And if the way he'd held her tonight was any indication, he was in love with her, too.

A soft smile curved her mouth.

And where there was love, there was hope.

Chapter Nine

Kara, dressed in shorts and a white shirt with blue stripes that she didn't bother to tuck in, hopped down from the veranda and went straight to the animal compound, just as she had every morning for the past two weeks.

She checked on the puppy first. Spike, as Kara affectionately called her, came running at her as soon as Kara walked into the large, shady pen the puppy had all to herself. Kara went down on her knees and let the puppy jump all over her.

Craig leaned over the fence and watched with a smile. "She's cute."

"Isn't she, though?"

"It's interesting to watch the way she is now. As she gets older, she'll get wilder."

Kara looked at him curiously. "Do you really think so? Even if she's raised here, among people?"

"The problem will be her unpredictability. You can never really domesticate wild dogs."

"But what about Sophia? A cheetah would seem to be more dangerous than a dog."

"Cheetahs are different. But then they're different even among other cats. For instance, you could never do with a lion what you do with Sophia. They have completely different temperaments. I mean, you can have a lion as a pet if you raise it from a cub, but you can never take its presence for granted the way you can with a cheetah. You can never quite trust a lion completely."

"And the baby rhino?"

Craig smiled. "Norman? It's hard to tell. I don't think I'd turn my back on him when he's full grown, though."

"It's really a shame he couldn't bond with the mother rhino we found."

"It happens."

"It's hard to imagine that they'll all be grown someday. I wish I could be here to see it."

"You can be. Just stay at Saragi instead of going back to Chicago with your sister."

Kara scratched the pup's head and rose.

He looked at Kara closely. "What's wrong?"

She busied herself fastening the pen gate. "Nothing."

"Judging by your face, that nothing certainly seems like something."

Kara stood for a moment staring blindly into the pen. "Craig, may I ask you a question?"

"Of course."

"Lucas left nearly two weeks ago to take the rhino to a sanctuary. When is he coming back?"

Craig looked just the slightest bit uneasy. "He had some other stops to make."

"I see."

"I'm sorry, Kara."

She managed a hint of a smile. "It's all right. You don't have anything to be sorry about."

"If it's any consolation, I think you're perfect for him and he's a jerk for turning his back on you."

Color flooded her cheeks. "I didn't realize I was so obvious."

"You don't exactly wear your heart on your sleeve, but I can see it in your eyes. And I meant what I said about your being perfect for Lucas."

"You know something?" she said softly. "I think so, too."

"Then you should tell him."

"It's kind of hard to do when he's not here."

"So wait for him."

"I can't."

"Why not?"

"Because Quinn and I are scheduled to leave tomorrow."

"Let Quinn go alone."

"I can't. She needs me."

"Oh," he said with a low laugh, "look again, Kara. Your sister might have needed you to lean on once, but she's just fine now. She's a lot stronger than she lets on. Stop worrying about her and take care of yourself for a change."

Kara thought about that without comment.

"And I'll tell you another thing. I think the reason Lucas is staying away so long is because you're here."

"But why?"

"Lucas has always avoided emotional entanglement, but never more so than since he got here. I don't think he sees his life in Africa as compatible with marriage and children."

"Great," she said dryly. "So what do I do now?"

"I don't know," he said softly. "Personally, I think the two of you should sit down and rationally discuss what's going on. The problem is that he might not even be back before you leave."

Kara sighed.

"You haven't done anything wrong."

"I have to get the elephants," she said in an abrupt change of conversation as she started walking.

Craig fell into step with her.

When they got to the elephant pen, the two babies, who by now almost considered Kara to be their mother, greeted her. She opened the gate and let them out.

"We're going to the river," Kara said. "We should be back in an hour or so."

"It's kind of handy having an actual body of water nearby, isn't it?"

"I can't believe how quickly the water came and how green the plain is all of a sudden."

One of the elephants nudged her from behind and Kara laughed. "All right, all right, I'm coming."

"I have some things to do," Craig said, "so I'll see you at dinner. Give some thought to staying here a little longer."

"I will. Thanks, Craig."

Kara started walking and the elephants walked together just ahead of her. As they rounded the house, Kara saw Lucas's Range Rover come to a stop near the veranda.

She stopped walking and watched as he climbed out.

Lucas looked at her also. "Hello, Kara."

"Hi. How's the rhino?"

"Fine. She's adjusting well to her new home."

"Good."

He inclined his head toward the little elephants who had turned around and were coming back for her. "I see you've made some new friends."

"I know. I wish I could take them home with me."

Lucas didn't say anything.

One of the elephants gave her a gentle shove in the direction of the river. "I'd better be going."

Their eyes met and held.

Kara got shoved again.

"Are you going to be here for a while?" Kara asked as she was being nudged along.

"Yes."

"Good. Maybe we can talk later."

Lucas didn't say anything. He just watched as she walked away from him toward the river with the two elephants.

When they got there, the animals waded in and splashed their trunks around. Kara waded in after them, scooping up water and throwing it on their backs, unaware that Lucas had followed and was leaning his shoulder against a tree, watching.

The elephants played a little rough and knocked Kara down a few times, but they always helped her up by extending their trunks.

One of them seemed to take great delight in filling his trunk with water and spraying Kara.

After about twenty minutes, the babies decided they'd had enough and clambered out of the water. They headed straight for home.

That's when Kara saw Lucas.

"You got wetter than the elephants," he said, straightening away from the tree.

"I always do, but I don't mind. They're fun to play with."

He walked toward her. "We need to talk."

"Yes, we do." She looked down at her soaked clothes, feeling at a distinct disadvantage.

"I've done a lot of thinking these past two weeks."

Kara's heart caught. She said nothing.

His eyes looked into hers. "You're so beautiful. You're a little clumsy, but you have a good heart."

She smiled and so did he. But Lucas's smile faded. "This is no place for you, Kara."

"But..."

"Let me finish. Maybe you'd do fine here for a few months or perhaps even a year, but in the long run you'd want to leave. I don't need any more grief in my life. Things are hard enough out here as it is. I don't want to let you into my life and heart only to lose you because you can no longer stand living out here."

"That won't happen."

"Of course, it will. And living here isn't something I can compromise on. I'm not going to be packing up and leaving in a year or two. I'm here for the duration. This is my home. This is my life. It's not yours and you wouldn't be happy here."

"I think I should be allowed to decide what would make me happy."

"That's because you're thinking with your heart instead of your mind."

"Sometimes that's the best way."

"Not this time."

Kara looked at him for a long moment. "Do you love me, Lucas?" she asked quietly.

"It doesn't matter."

"Of course, it matters. It means everything."

He shook his head. "No. What matters is that this is no kind of life for you. I've seen what it's done to other people. I've seen how it's hardened me. I don't want that to happen to you. You have such a loving heart. You deserve a lot more than life here can offer you."

"I want to stay with you."

"No."

"I love you."

He shook his head. "I'm sorry."

Kara had to fight back her tears. "Lucas, don't do this to me. To us. I know you feel something for me. I can see it in your eyes when you look at me. Don't turn me away because of some misplaced sense of chivalry."

"I don't want you here."

"But..."

He looked straight into her eyes. "I don't want you."

Kara felt as though she'd taken a blow to her stomach.

"Goodbye, Kara." He turned and walked away from her.

Kara stood there, watching him walk away from her. She wanted to run after him, but her pride had kicked in.

He didn't want her, much less love her.

She took a shaky breath and slowly exhaled. This wasn't the way it was supposed to happen. When you found the man you loved, the man you'd spent your entire life looking for, he was supposed to love you back.

Sophia nudged Kara with her nose.

Kara went down on her knees and hugged the large cat. "What do I do now, Sophia?" she asked.

Chapter Ten

The next morning, Craig drove them to the plane. Joe was already there, getting things ready. Without saying anything, the two men put the luggage inside.

As Joe climbed into the pilot's seat, Craig helped Quinn inside. Then, just before he hoisted Kara up, he put his hands on her shoulders and looked into her eyes. "You're making a mistake," he said quietly. "I know Lucas isn't exactly Lord Byron when it comes to expressing his emotions, but I can see what he's feeling every time he looks at you."

"He doesn't want me here. He made that very clear."

"Honey, Lucas wants what's best for you. Unfortunately what he thinks is best for you is going back to the United States and getting away from him. You know he's wrong about that."

Kara's eyes filled with tears. "Oh, Craig, I don't know anything anymore. And then there's Quinn. When I was talking to Lucas yesterday, I didn't even think about her. If I were to stay here, who would look after Quinn? She'd be all alone."

"Your sister," he said, lowering his voice, "is a lot stronger than she lets on. If you choose her over Lucas, you'll be making the worst mistake of your life. What you and Lucas have, whether my partner will admit it or not, is the start of a once-in-a-lifetime kind of love."

"Kara, come on. We'll miss our connecting flight if we don't leave now," Quinn called from inside the plane.

Craig held her arm. "Don't go."

Kara reached up and touched Craig's concerned face. "You're a dear man, and a good friend. But Lucas is the one who should be here asking me to stay, not you." She turned around and climbed into the plane.

As Joe started the engine, Craig closed the door and backed away. Kara looked through the window and raised her hand in a soft wave. Craig held up his hand as well, silently cursing his friend and partner for his stubbornness.

Kara leaned back in her seat and closed her eyes for a moment, but then turned her head and stared outside, watching as the plane turned around and then sped, bumping down the grassy runway until it finally lifted off and soared over the plain.

Kara sat forward on her seat and looked at the ground as the small aircraft dipped a wing and turned a half circle. They flew over the house and animal compound and out over the plain.

After about ten minutes in the air, she spotted Lucas's Range Rover, but no matter how hard she strained her eyes, she didn't see him.

Leaning back in her seat, she took a deep breath and slowly exhaled.

Quinn patted her knee. "It's for the best, believe me."

Kara didn't say anything.

Lucas was standing beside a tree when he heard the plane. He narrowed his eyes against the sun as he watched it fly over him. He kept looking until it was out of sight.

"Goodbye, Kara," he said softly.

It was a two-hour flight. Kara hadn't said a word the entire way. Her mind and pride were pulling her one way, her heart quite another.

Joe helped her down from the plane first, and then Quinn. Kara carried the shoulder bags, Joe got the suitcases, and the three of them crossed the tarmac to the small terminal where they were to catch their flight for Mombasa and then home.

"Here you go," Joe said as he set the suitcases behind several people who were already in line at the only ticketing desk.

"Thank you for everything, Joe," Kara said with a sad smile.

He hugged her. "You take care of yourself, and come back to see us. You, too," he said to Quinn.

"Thank you, Joe."

Kara watched him walk away.

"Don't look like that," Quinn said as she looped her arm through her sister's and squeezed it. "You'll forget all about Lucas Pierson and Saragi as soon as we get home."

"No, I won't," Kara said softly.

"Of course, you will. This entire episode was a momentary aberration in our lives. We should never have come here."

Kara looked at her sister. "We came here for you, and you have to admit that you're much better. Almost like your old self."

"I admit no such thing. I need you now just as much as I did before we got here."

They moved up in line.

"Did you hear what I said?" Quinn asked when Kara didn't respond.

"Yes."

"I never would have made it through Steven's death without you."

"But Steven's been dead for more than a year. It's time for you to get back on your own two feet and move on."

"What are you saying?"

"I'm saying that I can't spend the rest of my life being responsible for your well-being."

It was their turn. Kara lifted the suitcases into the opening next to the ticketing agent's desk. "Two tickets to Mombasa, please," she said. The rest of their travel arrangements were made, but they'd been told to handle this part separately.

"You've always been the stronger of the two of us. I rely on you just the way mother did when father died. And now that mother and Steven are gone, you're all I have in the world."

Kara watched as the ticketing agent wrapped a tag around the handle of her suitcase. "I can't do this," she said to Quinn.

"What?" Quinn said, her distress evident.

"I can't leave. Not now."

"But..."

Kara kissed her sister on the cheek and looked into her eyes. "You're my sister and I love you dearly. Nothing will ever change that, but I love Lucas, too. With all my heart. I can't just walk away from him."

"Kara, the man doesn't even want you! He told you so right to your face."

"Yes, he does. I know he does."

"But..."

"Please, please don't make me choose between the two of you, Quinn."

Quinn's expression suddenly softened. "I guess I'd better not, because I have a feeling I'd lose."

Kara didn't say anything.

"All right. Go to your Lucas. But when he breaks your heart, don't say I didn't warn you."

Kara hugged her sister tightly. "I love you."

Quinn nodded against Kara's shoulder. "I love you, too. You'd better get moving or you're going to miss Joe."

"Excuse me," Kara said as she grabbed her suitcase from the startled ticket agent just as he picked it up.

"Write to me!" Quinn called after her as Kara dashed for the door. "Let me know everything that happens!"

Kara hesitated at the door and turned back to her sister. Their eyes met for a long moment, then Kara flashed her a radiant smile and ran out the door.

Joe was already in the plane. He'd just started to taxi toward one of the two runways at the airport when he saw something out of the corner of his eye.

"Joe!" Kara screamed waving her arm wildly. "Stop!"

He turned the plane and taxied toward her before stopping. Kara threw open the door and stood looking at him, gasping for air. "I want to go back to Saragi. Will you take me?"

Joe's handsome face broke into a smile. "You bet I will." He hopped out and stowed her luggage while Kara climbed into the passenger seat.

"Ready?" he said as he got back into the pilot's seat and strapped himself in.

She looked at him and nodded. "Very ready."

"Let's do it."

As the plane left the small airport behind, Kara settled back in her seat. She was strangely calm. There was no question that she was doing the right thing.

Of course, Lucas might not be as happy to see her as she would be to see him, but that would change.

For two hours Kara sat there, lost in her thoughts. Joe didn't try to talk to her. He seemed to know instinctively that she wanted to be quiet.

"There's Saragi," he said finally.

Kara looked out the window at the familiar old house as the plane flew low over it and felt joy. In that moment she knew that she considered this her home, with all of its quirks and unpredictabilities.

As the aircraft circled out over the plain and came in for its landing, her heart rate picked up. She was expecting a confrontation, but she was ready for it.

No car came to meet them. She and Joe walked from the plane to the house. He set her suitcase on the veranda and winked at her. "Good luck."

"Thanks."

Kara stood in front of the door for a minute to collect herself. Then, taking a deep breath, she opened it and walked inside the game room.

Craig looked up from the newspaper he was reading and just stared at her for a moment. Tossing the paper aside, he strode over to her and pulled her into his arms. "I *knew* you wouldn't leave. I knew it."

"Then you knew more than I did." She looked around the room. "Where's Lucas?"

"I'm afraid he's not here."

"Where is he?"

"He came in a couple of hours ago, packed some supplies in his Range Rover and told me he'd be back when he got back."

Kara sank into a chair. "Oh, no."

"It's all right," Craig said, patting her shoulder. "What's important is that when he does decide to come back, you'll be here waiting for him."

"I'm sure that'll make his day," she said dryly.

"Kara, you didn't see his face when he came back here this afternoon." He looked at his watch. "You want to have some dinner? We already ate, but I'm sure we can dig up something in the kitchen."

"I'm not really hungry, thanks. I think I'm going to go for a walk and turn in early."

"All right. All I ask is that you stay out of trouble until Lucas gets back."

"I'll try."

"I don't handle stress well."

Kara rose from her chair and headed for the door.

"Uh, Kara, how did Quinn take your coming back here?"

Kara paused. "She seemed fine."

"She will be."

"I hope so."

Kara stepped onto the veranda and breathed deeply of the early evening air. It had a definite scent all its own.

She had to smile at herself. She'd been away for all of five hours, yet it seemed like months.

Something stood close to her, touching her hip. Kara looked down at the cheetah and rubbed her head. "Hello, Sophia. I'm home."

The cheetah went down the steps and headed for the rocks. She stopped after a few feet and looked back at Kara, waiting for her to follow.

And Kara did follow her.

She climbed the rocks more easily this time after weeks of practice, and sat on her perch to wait for the sunset. Sophia stretched out comfortably beside her.

"Lucas," Kara whispered. "Come home. Come home to me."

Lucas lay on the ground next to the fire, his hands behind his head. The sky was midnight blue, dusted with stars as far as the eye could see.

The fire crackled.

The animals made their night noises.

He'd been out on the plain like this, over the years, more times than he could count, for comfort; for peace; for solitude.

But tonight was different.

He'd never been so lonely.

How could a woman who'd come into his life so briefly, tear his world apart so completely?

How could Kara have planted herself so firmly in his heart that he knew she'd be there for the rest of his life?

And how was he going to get through that life knowing that Kara was out there, but not with him?

Lucas sighed, and it was a sound that came from deep in his soul.

Nothing would ever be the same.

Before Kara, his work here had been his life. It had filled all of his needs; taken all of his attention; drained him dry of emotion.

But now his life was divided into two parts: before Kara and after Kara.

And after Kara, nothing else seemed to matter much.

Lucas didn't question his decision in forcing Kara to leave. Not for a moment. He loved her too much to let her stay.

The question he had to ask himself was why he didn't leave with her.

It was that question that had driven him to come out here. And the answer was all around him.

There were some things in this world that were so important that sacrifices had to be made. He had to do what he could to save this place. He'd made progress in the years he'd worked on the Serengeti, but there was so much more to do, and so few people willing to do it. The survival of entire species depended on what happened in what little was left of the African wilderness in the next twenty years. Someone had to take responsibility.

He loved Kara. He loved her more than he'd ever imagined it possible to love.

He wished things could be different.

But they weren't.

Just because he'd decided on this life himself was no reason to force it on Kara.

And so he was here, looking at the sky, aching for what might have been; mourning what would never be.

Kara was sitting on her rock, just as she had every night since she'd returned, watching the sunset with Sophia beside her.

It had been a week since Lucas had gone, and she was getting worried.

As soon as darkness had completely fallen, Kara slid to the ground and walked to the house. Craig was sitting on the veranda rocking in a wicker chair.

"He should be back by now," Kara said as she sat on the top step and looked out at the plain.

"He'll come back when he's ready."

"Has he ever been gone this long before?"

"No."

"Doesn't that tell you something? Shouldn't you send someone out to look for him?"

"Stop worrying. It's not going to do any good. The man will show up when he's ready and not before." Craig got up from his chair and walked over to Kara. "It's been a long day. I'm going to turn in." He kissed her on the top of her head. "You should be getting to bed, too."

"I will. Good night."

"He's fine, Kara."

She nodded.

Kara stayed on the veranda a while longer, listening for the sound of an engine; for the sound of anything human.

But there was nothing.

She rose and went to Lucas's quarters. She'd been sleeping there so she'd know if he came in at night. Sophia went with her and curled up on an oval rug in front of the dresser.

Kara slipped out of her clothes and into one of Lucas's chambray shirts. She liked having something of his against her skin.

Climbing into his bed, she wrapped her arms around an extra pillow and hugged it to herself. She was tired, but it was difficult to sleep. If Lucas wasn't back by tomorrow, she didn't care what Craig said. She was going to go looking for him. Sudi and Ajani would help her....

An hour later, when Lucas parked his Range Rover next to the house, Kara didn't hear it.

He slammed the door of his car and walked down the veranda to his room. As soon as he opened the door, Sophia slipped out past him. "What are you doing in here?" he asked.

The cheetah disappeared around the corner.

Without bothering to turn on a light, Lucas tossed his hat onto the dresser and lay down on the double bed still fully clothed.

It took him a few seconds to realize he wasn't alone. There was the soft sound of breathing next to him.

Still lying down, Lucas reached over to the small end table and turned on the light. There beside him was Kara, her unruly red hair all over the place.

His heart caught.

"Kara," he said softly, rolling onto his side and touching her face, hardly daring to believe she was really there. "Kara, wake up."

Her eyes fluttered open. It took her a moment to focus, but when she did, her face filled with such unabashed joy that the question Lucas had been about to ask her died on his lips.

"You're all right," she said as she threw her arms around his neck. "You were gone so long."

Lucas wrapped her tightly in his arms. The fragrance of her hair filled his soul.

But then he regained his senses. Rolling Kara onto her back, Lucas raised himself up on his elbows and looked down at her, his eyes moving over her lovely face, examining every detail to see if he'd remembered her correctly. "What are you doing here? You should have been back in Chicago a week ago."

"I didn't go."

"Obviously. Why not?"

"Because I love you and I belong here, with you."

Lucas pushed her hair away from her face. "Oh, Kara, I told you this is no place for you."

She gazed into his eyes. "My place is wherever you are. I don't know how you could expect me to just go off and live my life as though we'd never met. You *are* my life. You're everything to me. And don't try to tell me that you don't feel exactly the same way about me. I know better."

Lucas pulled her back into his arms. "Oh, Kara," he groaned, "you feel so good."

Kara tangled her fingers in his thick hair as she buried her face in his neck.

"I love you," he whispered against her ear.

She lay back against the pillow and looked up at him, tears shining in her eyes. "Does that mean you'll let me stay?"

A corner of his mouth lifted. "It would seem that I don't have much say in what you do."

Kara smiled, but then her smile faded. She raised her hand to his face and touched his beard-roughened cheek. "What are you thinking?" she asked.

He turned his head and kissed the soft palm of her hand. "It's frightening, this power you have over me," he said softly. "You hold my happiness in those beautiful hands of yours. When I was on my own this past week, I resigned myself to never being really happy again. I thought I was going to have to spend the rest of my life with an unfillable void in my heart. And now, here you are. And even though I know I should send you away, I can't do it. I'm too selfish. I want you here, with me." He lowered his mouth to hers. "I want you," he breathed against her lips.

Kara opened herself to him like a flower, welcoming him inside. She ran her hands over his back and pulled him closer to her, but it wasn't close enough.

Lucas raised his head and looked down at her again. "I still can't believe you're here."

"Do you know," she said as she gazed into his eyes, "that I came truly alive for the first time in my life when I met you? You're everything I've ever wanted. Everything I've ever dreamed of. And the thought of trying to get through the rest of my life without you was more than I could bear. I had to come back, you see. I have to be with you."

Lucas rolled onto his back and pulled Kara into the crook of his arm, holding her close to his side, her head on his shoulder. He rubbed his cheek against her hair. "We'll get married tomorrow."

"What about tonight?" she asked softly.

He slowly moved his strong hand over the curve of her waist and brought it to rest on her hip. "Tonight," he said with a sigh, "we suffer."

Kara kissed the side of his throat, then raised herself on her elbow and started kissing her way down his chest as she unbuttoned his shirt.

When her hand was on the last button, low on his stomach, Lucas groaned and caught her hand in his. "I've wanted you so badly for so long, it's not going to take much to set me off."

Kara moved herself up so that she lay on the pillow beside him, looking into his eyes. "I need to be close to you. As close as we can get."

Lucas rested his lips against her forehead. "I need that, too. And we will. But first we're going to get married. We're going to do this right."

"You're sure that's what you want to do?" she asked.

He moved his head a little away from hers and looked into her eyes. “Quite sure. You mean too much to me to do anything less. I don’t want us joined for a night, or a week, or a month. I want us joined for a lifetime. When we make love for the first time, I want it to be as husband and wife.”

Lucas wrapped her in his arms and held her close.

And Kara knew that this was where she belonged. Here, with this man. Nothing else mattered.

For the first time in her life she felt complete.

This was definitely a holiday to remember.

* * * * *